PRAISE FOR .

The Dead I Kn...

'I have never read a book more gripping,
nor more triumphantly alive.'
– John Marsden

'What holds this superbly crafted narrative
at full throttle is suspense.'
– Christopher Bantick, *Weekend Australian*

Happy as Larry

'Funny, unsettling, sad, tragic . . .'
– Chris Thompson, *Viewpoint*

The Way We Roll

'As always, Scot Gardner nails it. *The Way We Roll* is
magic; it's dirty, rough, beautiful and understated magic,
full of hope, love and hugs.'
– Dani Solomon, Readings Carlton

Sparrow

'Scot Gardner has married two gripping tales of survival . . .
a cracking double-story full of guts and emotion.'
– Katharine England, *Adelaide Advertiser*

Changing Gear

'Scot Gardner explores the young male experience
with authenticity.'
– Joy Lawn, *Weekend Australian*

ALSO BY SCOT GARDNER

Changing Gear

Sparrow

The Way We Roll

The Dead I Know

Happy as Larry

The Detachable Boy

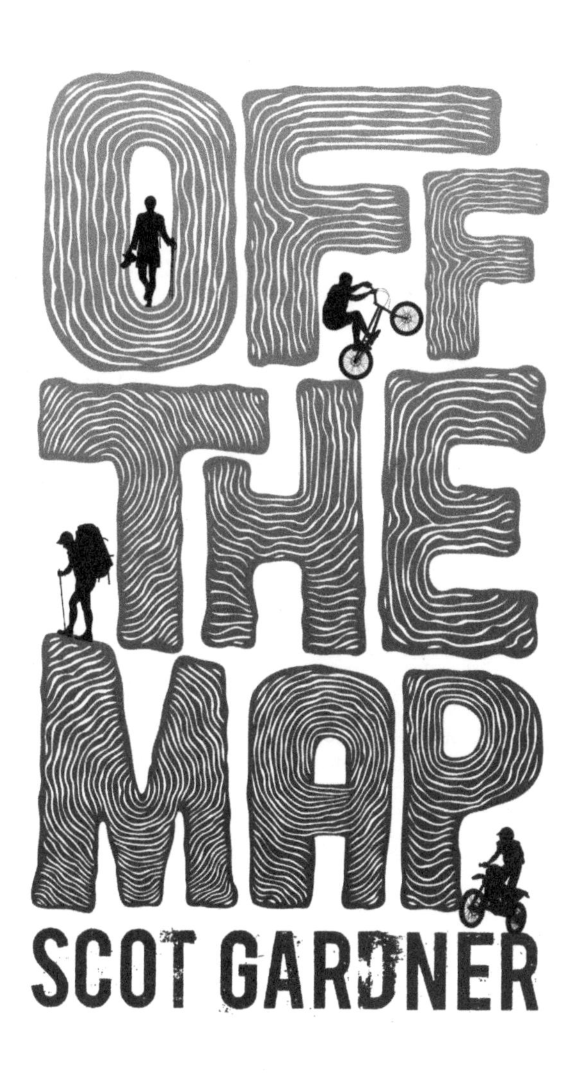
OFF
THE
MAP
SCOT GARDNER

ALLEN&UNWIN
SYDNEY • MELBOURNE • AUCKLAND • LONDON

First published by Allen & Unwin in 2021

Allen & Unwin
83 Alexander Street
Crows Nest NSW 2065
Australia
Phone: (61 2) 8425 0100
Email: info@allenandunwin.com
Web: www.allenandunwin.com

A catalogue record for this book is available from the National Library of Australia

ISBN 978 1 76087 710 1

Cover and text design by Debra Billson
Cover images by Shutterstock: lettering by jumpingsack; people by Vadimmmus
Set in 11.5/16 pt Adobe Garamond by Midland Typesetters, Australia
Printed and bound in Australia by Griffin Press, part of Ovato

10 9 8 7 6 5 4 3 2

scotgardner.com

The paper in this book is FSC® certified. FSC® promotes environmentally responsible, socially beneficial and economically viable management of the world's forests.

For Robyn

This is a work of fiction. The towns of Nerrima, Clarendon and Maybeline and the wilderness of the Magellan Peninsula don't exist in the real world, but they look a bit like the Australia I know and love. Similarly, the characters are imagined. More or less. *SG*

ANSWERS

Jael

The email that started it all didn't even arrive in my inbox. The fact I noticed it at all among the Lonely Lady/Viagra/Business Opportunity spam in my junk folder was one of those domestic miracles. A meaningful coincidence like knowing who's on the phone before you see the Caller ID, or like the time I turned on the TV and there was Luke Thomson videobombing. That made Luke the only person I knew that I'd seen on TV, and I'd just randomly turned it on and there he randomly was. Domestic miracle. Meaningful coincidence.

Anyway, the email was simple. The subject read 'Answers' and I wouldn't have opened it at all if I'd read the sender's name properly. It said it was from Luke Thompson. Luke and I had a thing in Year 9, but it never got sweaty. He's cute and capable of conversation, a good hugger, and he was brave enough to call Nathan Sharp a xenophobe to his face after we'd suffered through one of Nathan's barely masked racist rants. Luke is like a pair of shoes that feel nice in the shop, though when you get them home you never wear them. But that Luke Thomson has no 'p' in his surname.

So, I opened the spam email I *thought* was from a friend and it said: 'Hi Jael. Click HERE for ANSWERS. This is so cool!!'

I was on Mum's computer because my hard drive had died spectacularly on Monday – with plastic smoke – and I remember praying that the link wouldn't pop to a porn site. Mum was slumped in the lounge behind me, mostly watching *Millionaire* but I knew if the screen started filling with bare flesh, *that* would be the moment she'd casually glance over my shoulder and life wouldn't be worth living. Both my brothers, on separate occasions, had been roasted by Mum for surfing porn.

There was no gratuitous nudity. No smutty animation, just a white page and a single word in a scrolled Edwardian script.

Answers

I moved down the page and found two input boxes. One asked for my email address and the other was headed

'Please ask your question here'. At the bottom of the box was a button titled ASK. Okay, I thought. So it was one of those artificial intelligence things that spits out a response from a list based on the words in your question. I'd seen them before and had even asked a few questions, but the answers that came back were all wooden and lifeless. We still have a long way to go until AI moves from 'artificial' to 'intelligent'. Still, I did think the email was from Luke and that fact gave it weight. Luke was many things, but he certainly wasn't spam.

I entered my email address and stared at the heater thermostat on the wall while I pondered my question. It had to be something simple but juicy. I wanted a straight answer that didn't sound like horoscope gibberish.

What is my favourite colour?

I clicked the ASK button and it flashed through to an acknowledgement screen which said: 'Thank you for your question. Your answer will be emailed shortly.' There was a button centred below that. 'ASK another question?'

I refreshed my email – must have taken all of two seconds – and there was a new drop from Answers in the junk folder.

Subject: The Answer to Your Question

I opened the message and read the one-word response.

Magenta.

Okay. Lucky guess, but I have to admit, it did make me smile. And type another question. Something a little more personal. A little more abstract.

How many brothers and sisters do I have? ASK

Again, as soon as I hit refresh, the response popped up.

Subject: The Answer to Your Question

Two older half-brothers. One living, one dead.

The hair prickled on my neck and arms. I put my hand over my mouth. *Half*-brothers?

'What is it?' Mum asked.

'Nothing,' I said, a little sharply. 'Just a strange website.'

'Oh?'

'One of those artificial intelligence things.'

'Hmm.'

New question: *Where do I live?* ASK

Subject: The Answer to Your Question

12 Bellamy Street, Clarendon.

'Oh my god.'

'What?'

'The AI knows where we live.'

Mum groaned as she levered herself up off the couch. She put her hand on the back of my chair.

'You type your question, any question, and it emails you a response.'

She huffed. 'Be careful. Probably spyware.'

'It knew about Brodie.'

'What?'

'I asked how many brothers and sisters I had, and it told me I have two *half*-brothers, one living, one dead.'

The cursor blinked in the question box. I could hear Mum breathing.

'Really?' There was an edge to her voice. 'Who sent you the link?'

'This kid at school, Luke.'

'Luke who?'

I smiled then. A sly smile of satisfaction like when you crack a puzzle. Luke knew where I lived. Everyone knew about Brodie. The rest was just guesswork.

'Let's see,' I said, and typed my question.

Who is my father? ASK

Mum and Dad split up when I was four and we hadn't seen him since. He was the kind of secret my schoolfriends never knew about. As far as my secrets went, he was one of my deeper and darker ones. Or so I thought …

The response was instant.

'Who is Martin Davis?' I asked.

It was Mum's turn to put her hand over her mouth. Her pupils were big and shiny like someone had slapped her face.

'Who the hell is Martin Davis?'

'He was … I … Get off the computer, right now!'

Suddenly there was steel in my veins. If the bloke I'd been hating all my life wasn't my real father, maybe Brodie and Hayden *were* my half-brothers? I spun on the chair to face my mother, eyes afire. It seemed my rage had been misdirected all these years.

Mum sensed it. She stared back, then bowed her head. 'I'm sorry, love. I meant to tell you. I . . .' Her brow furrowed. 'How on earth did your friend know that?'

I clicked back to the question screen, my heart stumbling in my chest. 'I don't think it is Luke.'

Who are you? ASK

I have many names.

Where do your answers come from? ASK

The heart of hearts.

'What does that mean?' Mum asked.

I shrugged.

What are my mother's deepest darkest secrets?

She slapped my hand off the mouse and grabbed my shoulder. Her nails bit like a puppy's teeth. 'Don't you dare!' she fumed.

'Okay, okay,' I said, and held up my hands. That question could wait for another day. 'Your turn. What do you want to ask?'

She let my shoulder go. Her breathing was all choppy.

'Move,' she said.

I rolled the chair aside. She thought for the barest minute, then began typing.

Why won't my sister talk to me? ASK

'She's not *my* sister,' I said, but the AI responded as if it knew Mum had asked the question.

She blames you for the breakdown of her marriage.

'It can't be that simple,' she whispered.

'Sometimes it is. My turn.'

I sat there, staring at the screen, my mind aching with the possibilities.

'Hurry up.'

How can I stop global warming? ASK

The response was instantaneous again; only when I opened the email, it was seventeen pages long. There was no way it could have been typed in the seconds between sending the question and refreshing the junk folder. Maybe someone had asked that before? Maybe it was a stock response? I tried to scan through it, but the mouse scampered randomly over the page and I swore under my breath. I scrolled with the arrow keys. Step-by-step instructions. The names of people I needed to meet and things I needed to say to each person. Scientists, politicians, and that American actor, George Clooney.

'Read it later. My turn,' Mum said.

What are the winning numbers for Saturday's lotto draw? ASK

'Good one, Mum.'

She chuckled. When the email arrived, I wrote the numbers down as she read them out.

How can I stop the war? ASK

Again, the email response was as fast as a page can reload. Screen after screen of detailed instructions with passages in Arabic script and a map revealing the location of a parchment that would help every person understand the true essence of faith. The parchment would stride past all religions and give readers the capacity to imagine the world through other people's eyes.

'That's totally amazing,' Mum whispered. She wiped her eyes. 'It's a miracle.'

I couldn't take my hands off the keyboard long enough to wipe my own tears. They sailed down my cheeks and exploded on my lap. I clicked back to the original email.

It definitely hadn't come from the Luke I knew.

'What the hell? That's not how my friend spells his name.' The hair bristled on my neck and back. 'I don't know who this is from. I found it in my junk folder.'

'Who cares where it came from. Can't it just be a miracle?' Mum shoved me aside and her fingers scrambled over the keyboard.

Who killed Brodie? ASK

Killed Brodie? It was an accident. My heart was a drum roll as Mum fumbled to get the email open.

Hayden Turner.

Mum groaned. It came from deep inside her and was as mournful as a dingo's howl. It couldn't be. I read the name again. It wasn't possible ... was it? I remembered Hayden bawling at Brodie's funeral. He looked ugly and weird. I'd never seen him cry like that. Was he faking it? He must have been faking it. I remembered sharing the back seat of the car with him on the way home from the cemetery and silently wishing he'd stop sniffing. Pull himself together. He had no right to be that sad. Brodie had been *my* champion. *My* bouncer. *My* superhero.

Mum was typing again. I was too smashed to protest.

Why did Hayden kill Brodie? ASK

I grabbed the mouse. 'Don't, Mum. It doesn't matter. You don't want to know.'

'I already know,' Mum said, breathlessly.

Hayden was jealous of Brodie's confidence.

'That's just stupid,' I said, but it made perfect sense. Brodie shone. He'd crank the music up and we'd dance like crazies in the lounge while Hayden badmouthed us from the couch, arms crossed.

Mum nodded slowly, eyes closed as if in prayer.

I commandeered the keyboard.

Is there a heaven? ASK

You're in it.

Mum took the keyboard back again.

Is there a hell? ASK

You're in it.

With that answer still open, there was a faint electrical pop and Windows froze. The mouse stopped moving and a line of white pixels appeared across the top of the screen. Mum swore out loud and almost smashed the keyboard in her frustration.

'It's okay. We can restart,' I said, and gently shouldered Mum clear.

I turned the power off and on again. Windows wouldn't boot. It asked for a system recovery disk and then wouldn't recover. Mum was snarling through her teeth and pacing the lounge as I tried everything I could.

It was well and truly dark when Mum cracked it. 'I'm going to Gina's. I'll use her computer. What's your password?'

'I'm not giving you my password.'

'But …'

'I'll come with you.'

We rugged up.

Gina was all smiles until she saw Mum's expression in the gloom. 'What is it, Deb? You look hungover.'

'Worse. Can we use your computer? Just for a few minutes.'

'Of course. Come in.'

Mum stumped into the study. The chair shrieked as she dropped into it. Gina had been shopping on eBay before we'd arrived. Mum shook the mouse and found the login screen for our webmail.

'What's your …' She lurched out of the chair and made a sarcastic flourish with her hands. I sat down quietly and logged in.

'What is it, Deb?' said Gina. 'What happened?'

'A website. It's …'

The server rejected my password. I must have typed badly. I tried again, one finger at a time.

Invalid username or password. I retyped my address. I retyped my password. I restarted the computer.

Mum held her face in her hands. All the steam had gone out of her. 'It was a beautiful thing, Gina. A beautiful thing.'

'A website? I've seen some great websites but none that I'd mourn if I couldn't log on …'

Mum moaned. 'You have no idea. You could ask it *anything*. It knew the answer to anything. Everything. It was like a broadband connection to God.'

'Anything?'

'Absolutely anything,' Mum said, and rubbed her eyes. 'I asked who killed Brodie.'

'Oh my god,' Gina hissed. 'Oh my *god*. Why would you do that?'

Mum shrugged, and I was in.

'What did it say?' Gina asked.

Mum was hanging over my shoulder.

My heart sank.

My email account was empty. Wiped clean. Not a message in my inbox, not a single slice of spam.

'Where is it? Where has it all gone?' Mum whimpered. 'Oh my . . .'

'What?' Gina said.

'The link to the website was in my junk folder,' I said. 'All the messages were in my junk folder. All gone.'

'Can't you google it? What was it called?'

There were just over one billion websites containing the word Answers.

'What about the history on your web browser?' Gina suggested.

'We can't get the computer started,' Mum cursed.

'Call Dave,' Gina said, and handed Mum the phone. 'If it can be salvaged, Dave will do it.'

Dave reluctantly agreed to work on Mum's computer at that hour. We carted it around to his smoky garage in Tyler Street and he had the back off and the hard drive out in five minutes. He wired it into the exposed entrails of another computer, but the screen in front of him refused to acknowledge its existence.

'Sorry to be the one to tell you,' Dave said. 'She's fried. I can get you a new one for seventy bucks.'

Mum screamed. It was a long horrible scream for the

dead – hopes, hard drives and sons – and it made something metal in the shed ring in sympathy.

The silence that followed was bigger than the internet.

I hung my head as we trudged home. I felt wiped out, like I'd been running hot for too long; then the irony got to me. It was another one of those domestic miracles. Some freak of electronic nature had given us a window into something so much bigger than ourselves, and an equal and opposite freak of electronic nature had taken it away.

Hayden was home when we got there. He still had his work uniform on, and he smelled deep-fried. Mum just looked at him.

'What?'

She reached out her hand. 'I know it was you,' she whispered.

The statement seemed so vague, so random, but I watched Hayden buckle like he'd taken a blow.

'I know it was you,' she said again, but there was no anger or accusation in her tone. She took his hand and he folded into her.

'It was an accident,' he sobbed. 'I only meant to scare him. I didn't know he'd fall.'

With that confession, I had to revise the whole movie I had in my head about how my brother died. I'd pieced it together from what I'd been told – the scaffolding leading to the decaying roof of the old briquette works, the dare that got them there, the rain-slick metal. Maybe Hayden grabbed Brodie's shoulders and shouted, 'Saved you!', but he didn't. He killed him, but I don't think he meant to. Like the coroner said, it was an accident.

Hayden cried for a long time. Mum helped him into bed like he was a five-year-old. I made us hot chocolates. We sat in the lounge with the TV muted.

'Martin Davis?' I said.

Mum took my hand, kissed it. 'Could we talk about this another time? I promise I'll tell you everything you want to know. Everything. It's just –'

'*Half*-brothers?'

'After work tomorrow?'

The whole afternoon had been a Netflix binge about the dark corners of my life. Mum was saying it was time for bed and, for the first time in my entire life, bed sounded like a good idea. 'Promise?'

She licked her finger and drew an imaginary cross over her heart.

'It's a date.'

She kissed my hand again. And again. It got a bit cartoony.

'You know,' Mum said, 'I knew the answers to the questions before I asked them. Somewhere, deep inside me, I knew.'

'Your heart of hearts.'

Mum exhaled. 'Yeah.'

I nodded, but the more I thought about it, the less I believed. Answers had revealed so much about the world beyond my humble life. Mum was trying to play it down, so the miracle made some sort of accidental sense, so it didn't blow her mind, but my mind was already vandalised. My father wasn't really my father, my brothers weren't really my brothers. I'd seen beyond the flashing images of life. I'd caught a glimpse of what was beyond the set. I'd emailed the Director.

And there was nothing to show for it.

Nothing except a few numbers hastily scribbled on a scrap of notepaper.

THE TUNNEL

Alex

Boredom is the mother of insane stunts. I know that for a fact.

It was a grey day in the holidays. We were at Meat's place and we made a Frankenbike from the bits lying behind the shed. Nobody said, 'Hey, let's make a bike!' It just happened. Well, Meat and I assembled the bike, Nick watched from a safe distance, dressed as he was in vintage white tracksuit pants he'd scored on eBay. The monster we made had a standard mountain bike wheel on the back and a plastic scooter wheel on the front, wedged into a pair of racing bike forks that we had to massage with an old axe so they'd fit. High riser handlebars and a bell from a pink bike that Meat reckoned his sister didn't use anymore.

'Dude, lose the bell,' Nick suggested.

Meat shook his head. 'The bell's there to let other people know I have no brakes.'

Brring brring

I laughed. Nick called him an idiot – or words to that effect – and Meat stepped aboard the beast. The little wheel pitched the frame forward like he was in a permanent endo. He locked his elbows and made *phat* motorbike noises with his mouth.

He scootered down the drive – wobbling like a five-year-old without training wheels for the first time – hacked a U-turn and pedalled to the shed.

'Needs a lube,' Meat said. 'Other than that, it's awesome.'

'You need to give it a workout,' Nick suggested. 'I'll be cameraman. We need to give the bike a name. Think of a name, Alex.'

I looked it up and down. It *did* need a name. We gave birth to that wild metal child; we had to name it. The frame had a sticker on the side that used to say *All Terrain*, but flaky paint had made it *All Terra*. It was a short jump from there to Ball Tearer.

⤞

Meat and I took turns riding Ball Tearer around the court and up and down the gutters while Nick videoed us on his dumbphone. He reckons it's retro, but his mum told my mum that he can't be trusted with a smart one. We crowded around him and watched the grainy replays on the tiny screen, but the only movie that made us laugh was when Meat lost control and rammed the power pole.

'I have a challenge for you,' Nick said.

Meat crossed his arms. 'Bring it on.'

'Madigan Street.'

Meat threw back his head and laughed.

Madigan Street – the whole extreme-downhill kilometre of it.

➳

'You're mad,' I whispered.

'I know that,' Meat chuckled.

He was on the footpath, perched on the very top of the hill. Madigan Street fell away below him, empty of traffic except for Nick who was jogging to the bottom. Madigan Street has a *reputation* in Nerrima. Dana Quinn spent a whole maths lesson telling me stories about her street. She said it killed trucks – gave them heart attacks as they hauled their loads up its sheer face. She said if a car hit the bottom of the hill fast enough it would scrape on the road and sparks would fly. I've seen the deep grooves in the tar way down there. I believed her.

Nick waved.

Meat looked pale. I could hear him breathing.

'You don't have to do this,' I said.

'I know that. I'll be fine.'

'Why don't you start halfway down?'

He frowned. 'If I'm going to do it, it's going to be memorable. I'll either make it and have the video to prove it or I won't make it and I'll have the video *and* the scars to prove it.'

Nick was yelling. 'Come on! My phone memory is nearly full!'

Meat took a breath, kicked off and raced away.

'Woohoo!'

Brring brring brring

He dropped off the gutter with a clunk and took a line down the centre of the road.

I watched him and I ran.

Ball Tearer seemed stable and under control for the first half of the hill. I reckon he was at maximum velocity when the speed wobbles hit. Meat's legs shot out for balance, but the wobbles only got worse. He stomped his feet onto the road and the soles of his runners coughed and stuttered but the bike didn't seem to slow. The wobbles eased but Meat kept his shoes hard on the tar.

I know about friction. I know you can only use your feet as brakes for a certain amount of time until …

Meat swore and lifted his feet just as a black sports car crested the hill behind Nick, engine gunning.

Meat swerved, lost control, hit the gutter and somehow made it back onto the footpath.

If I hadn't seen the video of Meat's final stack a hundred times, I wouldn't have believed it was possible.

He wasn't on the footpath for long. Two zigs and one zag later, Ball Tearer's front wheel hit the metal barrier that stopped cars from driving into the creek at the bottom of the hill. It was like someone had pressed the 'Ejector Seat' button. Meat was catapulted over the handlebars and over the rail. A rolling tangle of limbs, crashing through branches and disappearing from sight.

The car roared past, oblivious.

Nick was still filming and swearing.

As the car crested the hill and the noise of its engine faded, I heard laughter.

'Meat?'

More laughter.

'You okay?'

'Yep,' he said. 'Woohooooo!'

Nick and I looked at each other and blew sighs of relief.

'Hope you got that on film,' Meat said. 'That was classic!'

'Got it,' Nick said. 'Come and check it out.'

'The only moving I'm doing for the next ten minutes is shaking,' said Meat.

I stepped over the rail. 'Come on.'

'I'm not going down there,' Nick said. He grabbed the front of his white jacket and frowned at me.

'Don't be a princess,' I growled.

I picked my way down to where Meat sat on a pile of broken reeds. He was smiling and shaking his head.

'Sure you're okay?'

'Fine,' he said. 'Check this out.'

He pointed to where the creek flowed under the road. It wasn't a bridge as such, just a pipe as tall as me.

'Yo!' Meat yelled, and it echoed down the pipe. It went on forever. A semi-fossilised shopping trolley lay upturned in the tunnel's open mouth, its ribs covered in chip packets and burger wrappers. A rank dribble of rusty water leaked from the base of the pipe. The concrete around the entrance was covered in black painted tags – mostly the name *Casper* over and over again but there were some stick figures being rude and a lopsided picture of a skull.

'Looks like Ball Tearer survived,' Nick shouted. 'Little buckle in the front wheel but other than that, it's fine.'

'Bring it down,' Meat yelled back.

Silence.

'He doesn't want to get dirty,' I said.

'Don't worry about your clothes,' Meat yelled. 'Come down. We've found a tunnel.'

'I've *seen* the tunnel.'

'Have you seen *up* the tunnel?'

'It just goes under the road.'

Meat was on his feet and we stepped past the shopping trolley into the throat of the pipe. Ten metres in, it became obvious that it went further than the other side of the road. The darkness and echoey silence came out to greet us. It rode on a cool, damp breeze that smelled faintly of rotting flesh. I don't mind admitting that my heart was banging hard and if Meat hadn't been there I would have bolted back into the light. Meat strode on confidently for another five steps then stopped. He shouted. It made me jump.

There was a loud metal crash. It made me cover my ears.

'There's your bike,' Nick shouted. He was a silhouette at the tunnel entrance, busily wiping something off his precious jacket. He walked to where Meat and I were frozen on the edge of the dark and started beat boxing with the echo. He's not the best beat boxer on the planet, but it did sound wicked in the tunnel. Meat started grooving, slapping the roof above his head and walking deeper into the abyss. I could see the reflectors on his runners and then he was gone, swallowed by the blackness.

'Meat?'

Nick stopped.

'Come on,' Meat eventually said. 'Grab the bike. We've got to check this out.'

'We haven't got a torch,' Nick said. 'We need a torch.

Come on, let's go. I have to get changed. We can bring a torch back. The bike will be okay there. Nobody will steal it.'

'I'm not worried about it being pinched,' Meat said. 'I want to ride.'

'In the dark?' Nick said.

'We can use your phone,' I suggested.

'Yesssss,' Meat said. 'Let's do this. Let's see where it ends.'

'It stinks in here,' Nick said. He took a can of deodorant from his jacket and sprayed the tunnel. 'I've got one of those headlamp things at home. It's bright as.'

'You won't get dirty in here,' I said. 'It's all concrete and stuff.'

I jogged to the entrance and untangled Ball Tearer from the trolley where Nick had dumped it. I wheeled it to Meat, and he patted the seat.

'Good beast,' he said. 'No bucking me off in here, or this tunnel will be your grave.'

I held the frame as he stepped aboard.

'Phone,' Meat demanded.

Nick breathed an exasperated sigh and handed Meat his phone.

'If you bust it you owe me fifteen hundred bucks, right?'

'Whatever,' Meat said. 'More like fifteen bucks.'

The phone's torch filled the tunnel with light and my eyes adjusted. Meat rode through the thin track of water in the bottom. Nick and I wide-legged it to straddle the creek and stumble-jogged to keep up. My heart was still doing its own beat-box thing, but I had a smile on my face. This was the sort of thing holidays were for. We were in the middle of an adventure. The tunnel curved gently to the right and within a minute the glow from the entrance disappeared and the phone was all we had.

Nick slipped. I heard the dull clatter of limbs and a tiny splash. He swore.

I laughed. I couldn't see a thing, but I knew what had happened. 'You okay?'

He swore again, louder this time, and Meat stopped.

'What?'

'Nick's had a bit of a fall.'

Meat backed the bike up and shone the torch on Nick. His white Dadas now had a brown, green and grey bum cheek. He wiped at the slimy mess but only managed to spread it further.

Meat chuckled.

'Give me my phone,' Nick grumbled.

'Why?'

'Just give it to me,' he shouted. 'I'm going home.'

'Come on,' Meat said. 'We're not at the end yet.'

'Do you know how much these are worth?' Nick bellowed. 'Three hundred bucks!'

'Yeah, well, they're dirty now,' I said. 'Going home's not going to make them any better.'

'True,' Meat agreed. 'Might as well see it through to its natural conclusion.'

'You guys owe me a new pair of pants.'

'Riiiiight,' Meat said. 'Whatever you reckon.'

'It's only drain slime,' I said. 'It'll wash off.'

'Phone,' Nick demanded.

'Come on, Nick. Don't be such a . . .'

'Look!' I interrupted. With the phone directed at Nick, the tunnel ahead glowed with a light of its own. 'We're nearly there.'

Meat gave Nick his phone and started pedalling towards the glow. I couldn't see a thing on the ground in front of me, but I jogged on behind Meat and Ball Tearer, each step a little leap of faith. The light had travelled a long way – I jogged for about two hundred metres before we found the source, but it wasn't the end of the tunnel.

The pipe opened into a chamber illuminated from above by a roadside drain. Roots hung from the ceiling like stalactites. The floor of the room was covered in crushed cans and plastic bottles. A metal ladder was bolted against the wall below the gutter. It was good to see the light of day, even though it was three metres over our heads.

'Oh, man, what stinks?' Nick said. He'd followed us anyway.

'Wasn't me,' I said, but I smelled it too. The pong of death again, only this time it was right in my nostrils.

Meat was off the bike and toeing at a hairy ball of something below the drain.

'Here,' he said. 'I think it's a cat.'

Nick gagged. He whipped his can of deodorant out and gave the cat carcass a good spray. Now the room stunk of dead cat *and* deodorant.

'How do we get out?' Nick asked.

Meat climbed the ladder and pushed at the manhole cover above his head. It didn't budge.

'Not that way.'

'Even if we could lift it, we couldn't get Ball Tearer out,' I said.

'Then we go out the way we came,' Nick said.

Meat dropped onto the layer of rubbish.

'We could. That's always an option. We're not at the end of the tunnel yet.'

'Check this,' Nick said. He poked at the rubbish with his toe. It was a used syringe with the needle still attached.

'There's another one,' Meat said, and I spotted a third when I bent to collect a tennis ball from the mess.

'Let's get out of here,' I suggested.

Meat climbed aboard Ball Tearer and pointed it in the direction of the unexplored tunnel. He looked at Nick. 'Coming?'

Nick's shoulders dropped and he turned to face the tunnel we'd been through.

'You can hold the phone,' Meat said. 'You can go at the front.'

'Why? So any crocodiles in the sewer get me first?'

Meat smiled. 'That's the general idea.'

Nick called him an idiot – or words to that effect – then crunched over the rubbish and into the new tunnel. Meat and I triumphantly fist-bumped behind his back. It wasn't over yet.

Chambers, drains and rubbish became more common as we ventured deeper into the pipe. Seeing the daylight every couple of hundred metres made the darkness between seem less threatening. Each new pile of rubbish offered treasures as well as disgusting stuff. I made quite a collection of tennis balls. Meat climbed ladders and tested the manholes, but they were all too heavy. He peered out the gutters and relayed what he could see.

'We're in Barkley Street!' he yelled. 'I can see the letterbox next door to my dad's place. We're nearly home!'

But in reality, we were a long way from his home. Unless we found a way out ahead, we'd have to backtrack to where the adventure started – all the way to Madigan Street.

At the next chamber, the pipe changed. The one leading out was smaller than the one we'd come through. The idea of having to bend down while we walked made my guts tighten. For the first time I felt like there wouldn't be another end, that the pipes would just keep getting smaller until we got stuck.

Meat didn't have to bend. Sitting atop Ball Tearer, he was a comfortable fit in the new pipe.

His eyes were wide. 'Now it's getting interesting.'

'Nope,' Nick said, flatly. 'Now it's time to turn back.'

'It's not a dead end,' Meat said.

'No, but it will be soon enough,' I said.

'Come on,' Meat protested. 'If the pipe gets any smaller than this, we turn around and go back. Promise.'

Nick took the lead again and I walked right behind him. So close that I kicked him in the heel. Twice.

'Ow! Watch what you're doing, Alex.'

'Sorry.'

'What's the matter with you? Give me some room.'

What *was* the matter with me? The fun was gone. The adventure wasn't an adventure anymore. You take the fun away and it turns into a sort of punishment, a torture. Meat had seemed like the big brave explorer until the fun went; now he looked like an idiot bossing us around, bent on self-destruction. I didn't want to be part of that. I was ready for the adventure to be over, but I knew it would take almost as long to get out as it had to get in.

I laughed with relief when we burst into another chamber and the light from the drain above revealed three small pipes. They were big enough to crawl through and they entered at shoulder height. This was the end. I knew we'd have to turn around. I found another tennis ball and a cigarette lighter that sparked but wouldn't hold a flame. I stuffed it in my bulging pocket anyway.

'Jackpot!' Nick hollered. 'Check it out!'

He'd found a leather purse. It was misshapen like it had been wet and dried but when he unzipped it, we all sucked breath.

It was stuffed with cash. Two hundred and sixty-five dollars, to be exact. There were credit cards, store cards and a driver's licence.

'Gail Edwards,' Nick read. 'She lives in The Don. Bellamy Street. Don't know her.'

'Give us a look,' Meat said. He took the card and studied it but shook his head. He handed it to me.

'She looks a bit like the hottie who works in EB Games in Central.'

'A bit,' Nick agreed, and his phone beeped.

'Message?' Meat asked.

I heard Nick swallow. 'Low battery.'

'You're joking,' I said. 'I thought the batteries on those things lasted for weeks?'

He nodded solemnly. 'You still have to charge them.'

In the brief silence that followed, we heard music. At least, it sounded like music, faint and buried in white noise as if the car radio wasn't quite tuned in. We had time to look at each other, puzzled, before the small pipe above Nick spewed water on his jacket.

'What the . . .?'

'Somebody flushed their toilet,' Meat chuckled.

The two other pipes and the drain above us began dripping.

'It's not the sewer,' I said. 'It's storm water.'

Meat swore, grabbed Ball Tearer and shoved it down the pipe he'd ridden in on.

I shoved Nick. 'Go!' I screamed.

'What?'

'It's raining!'

We ran and slipped and swore and bumped into each other. Nick's phone beeped like a dying bird. If it died, we'd be in total darkness. The trickle of water beneath our feet became a flow. We burst into the chamber where the pipe changed size and were instantly soaked by the waterfall that surged in off the road above. We ran, the current ankle deep and rising.

'Noooooo!' Nick howled. It echoed along the tunnel and was eventually drowned by the sound of rushing water. His phone battery had run flat and the darkness that swallowed us was complete.

'It's okay, Nick,' Meat said. His voice was as reassuring as my mum's in the black of a nightmare. 'We can do this.

We'll be okay. We just follow the water. One step at a time. Let's go.'

But the darkness was so total that we became disoriented every three steps. Nick was whimpering in front of me, Meat breathing hard behind. Rubbish floating in the water bumped at my calves and I thought I felt the dead cat. I screamed before I could stop myself.

'Let me in front,' Meat yelled. 'You guys can hang on to the back.'

Idea. I fished the cigarette lighter from my pocket and rolled the little wheel. The flash of sparks lit up the tunnel.

'Whoah!' Meat shouted. 'Again, again! Alex, you're a genius.'

I gave the lighter to Meat and he used it to crack holes in the darkness between the chambers. It was on the long last leg of the tunnel, when the water was pushing at my thighs, that the idea really came alight.

'Deodorant!'

Nick reluctantly parted with his can and Meat used it like a flamethrower, filling the tunnel with light, rolling forward in the dark then setting the stink alight again. It was Nick's idea to spray a patch on the wall of the pipe. Spray a patch, light it up and the concrete burned like a medieval torch for half a minute.

Meat swore. 'I dropped the lighter.'

Nick called him an idiot – or words to that effect – but by then, I could see the light. The rain had never felt so good on my face.

➳

Nick placed the purse on the counter at EB Games. 'Recognise this?' he asked the hottie. Her nametag said *Gail.*

'Oh … my … god!' she squealed.

She said it must have fallen out of her car. She gave him a hundred bucks. What was more surprising was that Nick gave Meat and me thirty-three dollars and thirty-five cents each. Just when you think you know somebody, they go and mess with your head by being generous!

➳

And Ball Tearer? The legend lives on. It rests beside the pile of bike skeletons at Meat's place. Nick posted the pixel-lated video of the stack. Look it up on YouTube and prepare to be slightly amazed. That was one insane stunt.

STRAY

Rhiannon

It's the random noises that get you.

You wouldn't think twice about them during the daylight hours but after the sun goes down, they become the soundtrack of a horror movie.

We all know how this is going to end.

I only have myself to blame. If I hadn't been so cocky the first time it happened, I'm pretty sure I wouldn't be here now.

I was thirteen back then. Mum was three hours away with Christie in Nerrima, and me and Dad went a bit crazy when it started raining. I've still got the bikini top I wore. I don't know why I've kept it – maybe for sentimental reasons – it hasn't fit me for years. Anyway, it wasn't normal summer rain we were dancing in. It rode in from the southwest like a grey-black army. It wasn't a storm – it was a *front*. A *weather event*. There was barely any wind and the rain fell apologetically to begin with.

Sorry, it said.

Excuse us, it said.

Pardon our wetness but we simply *must* kiss the ground.

But, as often happens with these things, the kissing got serious and the passion built until all the crazy was washed out of Dad's dancing and he stared across the paddocks looking worried. He collected his hat, pressed it on his wet head and ran for the big machinery shed.

'Where are you going?'

'I'll be back,' he bellowed.

I was under the verandah drying my hair. Next thing I heard the dogs barking on their chains and the John Deere starting up. The windscreen wipers were going flat out and Dad was waving with two fingers through the glass as the tractor sloshed past the house and onto the main track.

I mean, there was nothing unusual about that; that's just Dad. He does what needs to be done.

But three hours later, when he still hadn't turned up, I started wishing I'd got him to explain what he meant when he said he'd be back. Back today? Tomorrow? August?

He did eventually phone. It was after dark. The caller ID said SAT PHONE, so I knew he was in trouble. It meant he was out of range of the UHF radio; the satellite phone was for emergencies only.

'Dad?'

'I'm on the other side of Percy's Creek. The water's come up. Looks like I'll be stuck here for a couple of hours. Have to wait until the water goes down a bit. You be right?'

'Hours?'

'Yeah, you'll be right, won't you? Give Glenda and Barry a call if there are any problems. Anyway, I'd better hang up. I love you.'

'I love you too,' I said, but it was kind of a reflex. At that minute I felt abandoned. Glenda and Barry – our nearest neighbours – live three kilometres away and I knew they'd have storm problems of their own. Besides, Glenda never had kids, but she should have, if you catch my drift. She fusses like a hen and it creeps me out. It'd have to be a serious emergency for me to ring the neighbours.

No one died. It stopped raining and Dad got home just before 5 am.

I wish I'd cried then. Wish I'd seemed a little more vulnerable. That way it would've been easy to say that I didn't feel confident when they asked me this time if I'd be okay on my own.

I'm sixteen. I should be okay. This was planned for months. Christie had taken Mum to a day spa in Nerrima for her birthday and Dad had his fishing trip on the Magellan with Uncle Pete. I would have preferred fishing to day spa, but I didn't get an invitation to either. Someone has to look after the animals.

And this time when it rained, there was all the light and fury. The tail edge of Cyclone Francine had been terrorising the coast and she hadn't lost any of her punch when she arrived on our doorstep. The clouds churned and seemed to get grumpier by the minute, then bucket-sized drops started peeling the topsoil off the paddocks and dumping it in the creek.

The shed rattled like it was about to take off and the wind bumped against the windows like drunks. I hoped the dogs were okay. I thought about locking them in the laundry, but that would probably freak them out worse than the storm. They were working dogs, not pets. They had their old water tank kennels. I hoped the sheep would head for higher ground.

If it was a horror movie, the lights would have gone out, but we've got solar panels and batteries and a generator to use when the sun doesn't shine. If the power went out at home, that would be a serious emergency.

The phone was another story. The internet, normally as slow as a black-and-white movie, dropped out at about half past nine. I turned the modem off and on again, but it just kept flashing red lights at me. The phone was dead.

That's when the horror movie kicked off in my head.

Dad and Uncle Pete had the satphone.

With the landline dead and the internet dead, my only means of communication now was the UHF radio to the neighbours. That was a dodgy connection at the best of times. It hadn't been cyclone tested.

Everything's fine. I'm fine.

I kept telling myself that, but it did nothing for my heart rate.

Just a bit of a blow, that's all. Just a bit of rain.

Every so often a gust would drive the rain under the verandah and into the windows in a way that made it seem as if the glass was barely up for the job of keeping it outside.

I found some dim sims in the freezer and steamed them on the stove. Six didn't look like enough. Turned out ten was too many.

I closed the curtains in the lounge against the flashing night and watched *Aladdin* on DVD for the forty-ninth time – with the lights on and the sound up – but it couldn't compete with the mess going on outside.

I hope the dogs are okay.

As if on cue, a metal screech cut through the soundtrack. It went on for three seconds too long and ended with a crash I felt in my belly. I grabbed the big torch from the kitchen and tore open the curtains just in time to see the tail of a dog disappear along the verandah. The torch beam didn't reach the shed. All I could see was slanting rain.

Over the wail and clamour of the night, I heard knocking.

Knocking at the door.

It sounded desperate and weary.

Why hadn't I locked the doors? Why hadn't I grabbed the shotty from the gun safe? Why?

Because we live a million miles from anywhere and we just don't think like that.

I'd lived here for sixteen years and had never known the doors to be locked. The shotgun was for foxes and cats.

The knocking continued, but the rhythm grew jittery like the knocker had given up hope.

Was it the wind?

I crept to the darkened kitchen.

The knocking was coming from the back door. The kitchen door.

A blink of lightning didn't reveal a silhouette in the glass.

Not man. Not beast. Nothing.

Still, the knocking continued.

My heart rattled like it was driving over corrugations.

I stepped across the darkened room and flicked on the verandah light.

Nothing. Just the glint and shadow of rain.

The knocking stopped.

I tentatively opened the door and the wet breath of Cyclone Francine blew at my face.

And there, on the doormat, curled a dog.

Big dog. A German shepherd. One I'd never seen before.

'Hey,' I said, but it didn't respond. 'Are you lost?'

It leapt to its feet and, snarling, staggered into the rain.

It glared at me from the edge of the light.

I opened the flywire a crack and it rushed at me, barking explosively, hackles raised.

I backed inside and slammed the door, but it didn't stop.

I watched it through the glass as it snapped, wet-fanged and threatening, its whole body shuddering with the effort. Eventually, it barked itself to a growl then limped back onto the verandah.

It was skinnier than a farm dog, its muzzle grey and slack. It curled onto the doormat, its tail drumming on the flyscreen.

Psychotic. One minute it wanted to tear me limb from limb, the next its tail was knocking with puppy affection at the door. It whimpered like it wanted to come inside.

Not a chance. I wouldn't be going out there with that beast on the prowl. I locked the door and it growled again. I locked the front door as well. I tried to lock the sliding door in the lounge, but it had grown stiff with lack of use.

I watched the rest of *Aladdin* then went to bed around midnight, in my clothes.

I stared at the ceiling and the storm began to fade. I wondered if the dying wind meant I was in the eye of the cyclone, but the rain on the roof and the light show and the receding thunder lulled me into an uneasy sleep.

⇝

I woke early in a deafening silence. It seemed as though the birds had taken the morning off to assess the damage.

Three sheets of iron had been peeled from the roof of the big shed and I couldn't find them anywhere.

Patsy, our oldest kelpie, sat shivering beside the wall. Her water tank kennel had been blown into the paddock and bent out of shape overnight, but she seemed unhurt. I fed her and the boys, then let them off their chains. The boys cut laps of the yard, yapping like idiots. Patsy sat beside me watching them.

I patted her head, and she flinched. 'They're a bit crazy, aren't they, girl?'

There was no sign of the shepherd, not even a paw print in the mud. Maybe it had been a dream?

Freaking nightmare.

But under the light of a new day, the nightmare didn't seem as bleak and I started to wonder about the fate of the dog. It had travelled a long way. Maybe it had been dumped. Abandoned. The most recent chapter of its life hadn't been good. And I'd slammed the door in its face.

Still, it didn't take much to shake off those feelings. The dog was gone. Not my problem. My problem was where to start clearing up. I jumped on my motorbike and did a proper survey. The sheep out the back were picking through the stubble like nothing had happened, looking grey and damp but otherwise unfazed. Too many to count, but it looked like the full mob. I found those sheets of iron from the machinery shed about a kilometre from the house, totally bent out of shape and useless. I nearly dropped the bike a few times. The track surface was super slick, and I forged through puddles with my legs up but managed to get drenched just the same. I rode to Percy's Creek where Dad had been caught all those years before. I could see the rafts of sticks at the high-water mark and realised the creek had already receded ten metres. It shunted along like a gurgling brown goods train and I understood why Dad had decided not to drive the tractor across last time.

Back at the house, Mum arrived just after 2 pm. I didn't hear her car on account of the fact that I was using her chainsaw to cut up some fallen branches beside the stock-yards. The thing was blunt, and the chain was loose, but it eventually did what it was told. I killed the engine and Mum and I hugged. She smelled like lavender oil.

'You right?' Mum asked.

'Yep, fine.'

'I see we've got a new skylight in the shed.'

'Patsy's kennel got a bit of air, too.'

'What's that?' she said and pointed to a lump in the paddock.

A brown furred lump.

I can't really explain why, but my heart sank when I recognised the form.

I jumped the fence and ran, but stopped a few metres short.

It was the shepherd, all right. The rain had pressed its fur flat against its ribs.

'Hey,' I said, but it didn't move, and a sadness washed over me like the frigid waters of Percy's Creek.

The eye I could see was partly open, blue with age and death.

I knelt on the damp earth beside its head and rested my hand on its neck. It didn't smell dead yet, only like wet dog.

Female.

A matted ridge of fur marked a line where a collar used to live around her neck.

She'd been somebody's pet. She'd been somebody's friend. She'd spent her last night on earth wet, frightened and alone, navigating in the dark through a cyclone.

Is it any wonder she was growling?

And I thought *I'd* been scared.

All she'd wanted was a little bit of refuge and I hadn't even given her that.

Sure, she was old, and she may have died anyway, but I couldn't help thinking that if our roles had been reversed she might have shown some compassion towards me in spite of her fear.

I dug a grave for her using the bucket on the loader. It was in the corner of the paddock beside the old river gum. I carried her there in my arms. She was a lot lighter than she should have been. I backfilled the hole with a shovel, picked a couple of canola flowers to lay on top, and I knew that if I had to face another storm like that on my own, I'd wedge the doors open.

THE WAVE

Martin

Sometimes love is catastrophic. They don't mention that in popular culture. It deserves a meme, but it's probably hard to match with an image of a cute puppy, kitten or panda. It might need an aftermath pic – cyclone, flood, tsunami. One where the victims have plenty of warning to vacate their lives while love does its thing. Here's me, knee-deep in mud, picking up the pieces. My life's a mess. Love did that.

It arrived out of blue skies and I nearly drowned under all the tropes and clichés. Hearts fluttering, birds singing, wolves howling.

Wolves howling?

I waved to Pippa Hansford when we first met. We made eye contact for the first time in our lives and I waved and smiled. She grinned and waved back, like 'Oh, there you are. Finally!'

It was the debating semi-finals. Pippa and her team from St Hillary's in Maybeline had been on the bus since before school ended to make it to the Nerrima Performing Arts Centre for the 6 pm start. Six pm? Maybe the organisers grew up, like me, debating their sister and parents over dinner. I was hungry. The other St Francis boys had bought Macca's on their way down. Mum offered to bring me something from home but I told her it's good to debate on an empty stomach. Mum was sitting with my sister in the centre of the theatre. Amanda's uneven auburn braids stuck in the air like bent antennae. They were good cinema seats. I hoped they'd enjoy the show. I found a veteran apple in the bottom of my bag. That would be enough to keep my blood sugar up and my brain firing, but a little bit of hollow in my belly keeps me keen. Wanting for food pairs nicely with wanting for victory.

Victory was never going to be as simple as a trip to Macca's that evening. Pippa Hansford was St Hillary's second speaker. She spoke straight after me and she ate my arguments alive, with a smile on her face. Her glasses and her braces glinted under the stage lights. She called me her 'esteemed colleague in the affirmative' and my face burned.

We lost the debate soundly. We lost, but I won: I shook hands with Pippa Hansford, and we swam in each other's eyes for this tiny little infinity.

'Martin Jones,' I said.

'I know,' Pippa Hansford said. 'I'm Pippa.'

'Of course.'

'I like your hair.'

'Thank you. Dad says it makes me easy to find in a crowd.'

'Unless it's a crowd of crazy yellow-haired surfer dudes.'

'True. That would be problematic.'

I sent her a friend request and she'd DM'd me while we were eating dinner. It was a red squid emoji and I have no idea what it meant but it rang through me like church bells and made it hard to listen to what Amanda was saying. She was deconstructing my performance like a good debating coach. I nodded, but in my head I was composing a reply to the red squid. City building? Mountain climber? Goat? I finally settled on a pirate flag. Her response was instant.

Argh.

Argh, I replied.

And then, later, I got another message. *Debate topic: Waving to complete strangers is healthy. First speaker for the affirmative, Martin Jones. Three sentences. Five minutes. Your time starts now.*

She really did know my name.

I said goodnight to Mum and prayed she wouldn't feel my heart thumping when I hugged her.

Amanda knew something was up. She stopped brushing her teeth to frown at me in the mirror.

'You okay?' she gargled.

'Of course,' I said. 'Fine and dandy.'

'Dandy?'

'Dandy.'

'That's ominous.'

'What?'

She raised her eyebrows but said nothing. She spat, rinsed, air-hugged me and bid me goodnight.

I sent my response with twenty seconds to spare.

Waving to strangers is a powerful tool for acknowledging the humanity in another. It is a sign of goodwill. A wave is silent, ancient and universal communication that transcends language and cultural boundaries.

Her rebuttal arrived four minutes and forty seconds later.

Waving to a stranger may acknowledge the humanity in another but it can make people suspicious. It is often used as a sign of goodwill, but it is also the currency of con artists and hucksters. While a wave can transcend language and cultural boundaries it can also engender a false sense of community.

I lay on my bed rereading that and sinking. I thumbed a couple of replies but didn't send them. In the end, all the posturing fell away and there was only naked truth left.

I knew you. We'd never met, but I knew you.

Her reply arrived two breaths later.

Weird, huh?

Yep. Weird. Good weird?

I'm here aren't I?

What have I missed?

Missed?

Your life. Tell me a story.

The ellipses rolled like she was typing. They did that long enough for me to get into my pyjamas and under the covers.

A story like that should be told in person.

Maybeline was only three hours away, but it was also three hours away. We wouldn't be catching up for coffee – did Pippa even drink coffee? – after school.

The holidays are four weeks away, I messaged.

What are you doing on Sunday?

I typed *Nothing*, but I didn't send it. I knew St Hillary's was a Catholic school, but lots of non-Catholics go to Catholic schools. Even though there's nothing quiet about our church, I'm quiet about my faith. In the end it was my dad's voice in my head. 'Remember to be true.'

Church.

Me too, was Pippa's reply, and I worried Amanda might hear my sigh of relief through the bedroom wall.

Finished by 11, she added.

Can you get to Nerrima?

Can you get to Maybeline?

I checked the train timetable, my account balance and the expiry date on my student card.

Yes.

I'll ask my mum.

My mum was in bed with her headphones on watching something on her iPad. She tapped the screen and popped an ear.

'Okay, love?'

I leaned on her wardrobe. 'I've met a girl.'

Her eyes flashed and a crazy grin stretched her face. 'The St Hillary's girl from the debate?'

'How can you even know that?'

Mum touched her nose. She patted the bedcovers beside her, and I sat.

I told her everything. I remembered to be true.

'If it's okay with Pippa's mum, would you mind if I took the train up to Maybeline after church on Sunday?'

'Wow, this is really sudden, Martin. Can't you just video chat?'

I shrugged. 'There's something about her.'

She patted the back of my hand. 'Let's talk about it some more in the morning.'

I opened my mouth to protest – all I wanted was a simple yes or no – but I caught myself. I nodded and kissed her cheek.

My mother would like to speak to your mother, Pippa messaged, then my phone rang.

I couldn't breathe, but I answered it. 'Hello?'

'Hi. It's me. Could my mum talk to your mum?'

'I ... I'm not ... Yes, of course. Just hang on a minute.'

Mum rolled her eyes, popped an ear and paused her show again.

I handed her my phone. 'Pippa's mum,' I mouthed.

Mum scowled but took the phone.

'Hello? Oh, hi. Pippa's mum? Hi Bec, I'm Angela, Martin's mum.'

I left the room. I sat on the toilet with the lid down and the door shut. I rubbed my face. Yes, it was all happening fast, but I'd never been so utterly blindsided. Maybe this was love's normal speed? My fingers tingled and my lungs wouldn't fill until I put in some conscious effort. *Breathe.*

Mum called me. I half-flushed the toilet for effect and wiped my hands on my pyjama pants before taking my phone. Pippa and her mum had gone.

'She sounds lovely,' Mum said. 'They're only a couple of minutes' walk from the station. Give them a buzz when you get there.'

I hugged her head. She patted my shoulder.

'Best behaviour.'

'Of course,' I said.

⤞

Pippa waved. She was waiting on the platform at Maybeline and she'd seen me through the window. I was going to write that my heart skipped a beat but that's not an accurate portrayal of the state of my internal organs. There was lung stuff going on – they felt like over-filled party balloons – and my bladder was threatening to drop the floodgates. Should we hug? Shake hands? I didn't know the protocol and I'd left it too late to google. Pippa didn't leave anything to doubt. She was jiggling on the spot as I stepped off the train and signalled her hugging intentions with wide arms and an even wider smile. She'd straightened her hair and it smelled toasted and clean. The hug was over in a split second, but it eased the pressure on my lungs and bladder. She offered to carry my satchel, so I let her. She asked about the trip and I told her the train was packed. I told her about the man opposite who snored into his oxygen mask the whole trip. I thanked God for noise-cancelling headphones and Claude Debussy.

She frowned. 'You listen to Debussy?'

I shrugged.

'I've never met anyone else my own age who listens to Debussy by choice.'

'Dad's fault. Pat's a sucker for the early Impressionists.'

Pippa frowned. 'Your father's name is Pat?'

'Patrick.'

'Mine too!'

Turns out her father – Patrick Hansford – also worked at Bellavale like my own dad, which wasn't such a huge coincidence because half of the working populations of Nerrima and Maybeline were employed by the power station somehow. Patrick's not exactly the most exotic name. Her dad was an engineer in the mine; my dad's a unit controller in the station itself. Like most Bellavale employees, they worked two weeks on, two weeks off. And they both had side hustles they worked on their fortnights at home. My dad tests electronic appliances and tags them when they're safe. Pippa's dad did something called non-destructive testing which she described as making sure concrete was strong without destroying it. Both our dads were always working. I might get to meet Pippa's dad as he was due home for dinner.

She looked like her mum, or maybe her mum looked like her – glasses *and* braces. All that gleaming metal in her mouth made Bec look more like an older sister. She'd straightened her hair too. We shook hands and she lingered, her head tilted. It was a weird look, but her words never left the script.

'So nice to meet you, Martin. Welcome. Please make yourself at home.'

'Thank you, Mrs Hansford.'

'Please, call me Bec.'

'Thank you, Bec.'

Pippa's sisters came flapping into the lounge like pigeons. Molly, the thirteen-year-old, had perfect teeth and a yellow-blonde bob. She wore three-quarter-length navy overalls and rainbow socks. Bianca, twelve, wore leopard-print tights and bare feet, her auburn locks in uneven braids. I noticed those things because the whole scene felt weird. Déjà vu. I felt like I'd watched this episode before, all the details seemed familiar, but I couldn't remember the story. Molly and Bianca waved their greetings and I waved back. Maybe we were all robots?

My internal organs no longer had individual personalities. I'd become a skin bag full of confused soup. Some part of me longed for the comfort of science fiction. Some part of me longed for a primary school ending like 'and then I woke up', but sometimes the world is weirder than our imaginings.

On the outside, we played Monopoly. We rolled the dice, formed and shattered allegiances, laughed hard and authored polite ways to curse our misfortune. On the inside, my organs regrouped, and I realised – when I found myself at the kitchen sink filling glasses for everybody – that I'd taken Bec at her word and made myself at home.

'You can have my bed,' Molly said.

'Pardon?'

'You can have my bed. I'll sleep on the couch.'

'That's very kind of you, Molly, but I have school in the morning. In Nerrima.'

Her shoulders slumped and I checked my phone. Eighteen minutes until my train. Pippa would have won the game. It may have taken another eight hours, but she was lucky, generous and ruthless when it counted. We divided our cash and properties so that Molly and Bianca could play on. Pippa insisted on carrying my satchel. I asked to use the toilet and when I returned, Pippa's father was home.

The final piece of the jigsaw. His eyes flashed when he recognised me. Other than that, he didn't miss a beat.

He had Molly under one arm and Bianca under the other. They clung like lost chimps and he kissed their heads until they let go. Molly's yellow surfer hair. Bianca's uneven auburn plaits.

My skin crawled. I felt starved for air. I couldn't take my eyes off him.

We shook hands like perfect strangers and his secret became my secret.

'Martin, is it?' he said, deadpan. 'Pleased to meet you. I'm Pat.'

My words dried up. It wasn't sci-fi or a hallucination; it was a horror story and a true-crime thriller.

Remember to be true?

'We have to go,' Pippa said. 'Or Martin will miss his train.'

'It's pouring out there, love,' Pat said. 'Jump in the car and I'll drive you.'

I hugged Pippa's mum and sisters – Molly kissed my cheek – and I knew I'd never see them again.

At the station, Pat produced an umbrella from the boot and the three of us huddled under it as we scampered up onto the platform.

The train pulled in.

'I'll text you,' Pippa said, and we hugged.

I found a seat.

The conductor blew his whistle.

The doors beeped as they shut.

Out the window, Pippa clung to her father. The umbrella was low over their heads.

The train sounded its horn and we began to move.

Pippa waved and I waved back.

Pat's eyes locked with mine and his lips moved. I heard his voice inside my head.

'Your mother can never know.'

I sat on my hands and stared out the window as the evening lumbered home. I listened to Debussy's *La Mer* and the sound of my heart being torn apart on the rocks.

Of course my mother could never know. Amanda could never know. Pippa, her mum and her sisters could never know. It would derail our lives.

All of them.

I loved my father too much for that.

THE KID

Chloe

My dad has lived in our house since he was a kid. Our driveway is famously steep. They even call it Veno's Hill. We can see the ocean from the verandah on clear days. It's one thousand, six hundred and seventy-three metres from our front door to the bus stop and, except for the flat section near Motorbike Man's house, it's all seriously downhill. It takes twenty-two minutes to walk there in the morning and thirty-six minutes to drag myself home in the afternoon. It's December and I have two weeks left in Year 8. I haven't missed the bus – accidentally or on purpose – since the nineteenth of September, which is a record for me. I wish I could say – like my maths teacher Mrs McLaren said in my report – that it was due to 'Chloe's high levels of enthusiasm', but it's not. I just like to leave home before the silence freaks me out.

There are a few distractions on the way down. If he's near the fence, I'll say good morning to Hamish, the Highland bull calf who lives at the next property. I scratch his ear through the wire, and he tries to lick me with his crazy-long purple tongue, then he trots beside me to the edge of his paddock. I have to look away at that point – his long eyelashes and his sad sad eyes have made me miss the bus before. 'Muh,' he bellows. I think he loves me.

The next distraction is two driveways further on, on the opposite side of the road, at the letterbox that says *Hunter-Davidson*. Charlie's waiting. I thought he was a baby when he arrived, but that was a year ago and he hasn't gotten any bigger in the body, though his horns seem sharper. I'm the only person in the world who plays with him, so I named him Charlie. I don't know the Hunter-Davidsons. Well, I've seen them – he has a big red beard, and she's a policewoman – and they wave as they drive past but we haven't spoken actual words. Charlie is a better name than anything they could make up.

Charlie's chained to the letterbox and he converts all the grass and leaves he can reach into little green marbles. He has an ash tree for shade and an old ice-cream bucket for water. He's a lonely goat with emotional problems. Some mornings he rattles over for a pat and nibbles my fingers with his velvety lips. Other mornings, he rears up on his hind legs and tries to crack my skull open with his. I'd have to get down on all fours for him to have a chance of hitting his target. I can never tell what sort of mood he's in until I'm actually in range. Maybe it's just goaty play-fighting he wants, but I'm a girl, not a goat. And he's a goat, not a girl, so I love him as he comes.

The last time I saw Mrs Hunter-Davidson, she didn't see me. I was on my way to the bus with time to burn and Charlie was in a good mood. I fed him a handful of grass and crouched with him under his tree. Their house is a hundred metres from the road, but I could hear them shouting. I couldn't understand what they were saying, but they sounded like dogs fighting. It made me feel sick. Glass smashed, doors slammed, and Mrs Hunter-Davidson's car screamed along the gravel drive and onto the road. She didn't stop to look for traffic and the tyres became scribbling howling smoke dragons as she hit the tar. Are police even allowed to drive like that? Fight like that? I hurried down the road as if I hadn't seen or heard anything, but five minutes later, when Mr Hunter-Davidson's car burned past, my breathing was all weird and my heart blatted in my chest like it did at night when the house was dead quiet and I could hear the silence through my pillow.

I wish I'd missed the bus. The day was already hot. The bus was hotter. We played games in the gym for PE and that was hotter still. Someone had taken the aircon remote from our English room so we went to the library and played (word) games there, too. When the hot bus dropped me off onto the hot road to walk the one thousand, six hundred and seventy-three metres up the hill, I thought – briefly – that it might be easier to lie down on the tar and wait for a truck to put me out of my misery, but Mum arrived. She'd never been home from work this early before. She popped the boot for me. She didn't say anything as I sat beside her, just flashed the biggest fakest smile. The car laboured up the hill, the radio played a song I hated, and the air-conditioner blew its warm breath on my face. I couldn't bear to look along the Hunter-Davidson's driveway, but I saw Charlie lying in the sun beside the letterbox. Idiot.

Dad cried. He hugged my head at breakfast and told me that he had to leave. That he and Mum loved me, but they couldn't live together anymore. I wasn't surprised. The silence had hurt my ears because I knew it was the sound of my family rotting from the inside out. I didn't know what to say. I didn't know what to do. I patted his arm and collected my schoolbag. They argued silently about who would take me to the bus stop. I told them I'd be fine, but I wasn't.

Hamish waded with his mum in the dam on the other side of the paddock. Charlie was still lying beside the letterbox, his eyes closed.

'Charlie?'

I dropped my bag and sank to my knees.

'Charlie?'

I patted his head and his ear twitched. His chain had tangled around his legs. He'd been bound like that all day and all night. He was breathing – panting – but his head flopped as I rolled him on his side and his horn dug into the soil. I unclipped and untangled his chain then carried him to his ice-cream bucket, but the bucket was empty. I left my bag on the road and jogged with him along the Hunter-Davidsons' driveway. There were no cars. Nobody came when I called. Nobody came when I squealed and kicked the door. I found a hose out the back and a plastic bucket. I laid Charlie on a shaded patch of mulch. The bucket shattered as I tried to fill it, so I set the hose at a trickle and wet Charlie's legs, his head, his velvety lips. No thirsty tongue flicked out to collect those drops, instead his panting turned to shivers. I cradled him on my lap until the shivering stopped, until the panting stopped, until he died in my arms.

BAD BILLY

Mason

Boots nudged my knee with hers. 'Tell them,' she whispered.

I played dumb.

She butted my leg again, insistent.

I shot her a look, but the firelight worked like a forcefield. I was surprised she remembered my story. We were in primary school when I told her. Year 5, maybe? She was tired. She gets pig-headed when she's tired. All five of us were tired. Tired and hyped and trying to stave off the darkness with freaky stories around the campfire. It was the last night of our hike. Tomorrow, we'd be back in civilisation and these guys wouldn't be seen dead with the likes of me and Boots.

Chen grabbed the peak of his cap. 'I've remembered another one.'

Dana gave a little cheer and clapped her gloved hands, which made Chen grin. It feels good to please the gods, and Dana was the high goddess of Nerrima High. By popular vote.

Tariq tutted. 'Not you, Chen. You're shit at this. Give up while you're behind, man.'

Dana shushed him. 'Go, Chen.'

'Go, Chen,' I echoed.

Boots snorted and crossed her arms.

'Last summer holidays I stayed at my auntie's place in The Don, right, and she doesn't care what time we go to bed, so me and my cousins had these all-night gaming sessions. Anyway, three days and nights of gaming and I'm starting to get a bit delirious, right? It's about three o'clock in the afternoon and I hit the wall, like seriously tired, and I faceplant on the bed. It was still daylight when I woke up, but I couldn't open my eyes. I'm lying face down, right, and my arms are underneath me and I can't move them. I start freaking out and I'm trying to yell for help but there's no sound coming out. I'm completely fucking paralysed.'

Dana's hand was on her mouth.

'I don't know how long I was stuck like that. I honestly thought my brain was fried, that I'd be locked inside my head forever. Then I hear this evil chuckle behind me, right, like full-on horror movie shit, and I'm thinking I'm about to be arse-raped by a demon and there's nothing I can do about it.'

'You would have loved it,' Tariq said.

Dana shoved him. 'Shut up.'

Chen shivered. 'I don't know about that. It was fucking scary.'

'Maybe at first, but eventually you would have loved it,' Tariq said.

'That's my worst fear,' Boots said.

'Being arse-raped by a demon?' Tariq said. 'I thought that would be on your bucket list, Boots.'

She ignored him. 'Being locked inside your head and unable to move. That's the cruellest sort of prison.'

'True, that,' Chen said. 'But then I hear my auntie shouting at my cousin in Mandarin and it's just stupid shit like he can't fold his underwear properly, and the spell is broken. I'm awake and the demon's gone and my limbs can move again. I'm puffing like I've run a marathon.'

'Scary shit,' Dana says.

The night went silent, like the gap between album tracks.

Boots leaned in and shoved a burning log. A fountain of orange sparks escaped into the night.

'Mason has a story,' she said.

I kicked her foot and for a few seconds it was like nobody heard or cared.

'Go, Mason,' Tariq said.

I don't think I've ever heard him say my name. Maybe he *could* see me after all? That was disconcerting. It wasn't just Tariq watching me, either. Boots had set me alight and now I was the fire they were all staring at.

'When I was five, my nanna got sick and I went to the hospital with my mum to visit her. The old hospital, when it was still on Foster Parade. My nanna smelled bad, like she was rotting inside, so I snuck out and played with this wheelchair kid I met in the waiting room. He called himself Bad Billy. He was maybe twelve or so and he'd lost both his feet in an accident. He taught me how to play draughts and then flogged me mercilessly. I never won a game, but I kept coming back. He didn't treat me like a little kid, you know? My nanna was in that hospital for more than a month. Mum's friend, Terri the nurse, told us to say our goodbyes. We all thought she was going to die.'

Dana squeaked and shot to her feet. In a flash, her tracksuit bottoms were around her ankles. She swiped at the back of her thighs with her gloved hands.

'Orright!' Tariq said. 'Now it's a party!'

Dana spun to inspect her legs in the firelight. 'Something bit me.'

'There,' Boots said. 'On your pants. It's an ant.'

'Ha!' Tariq said. 'Ants in your pants, hey Dana?'

'Ant,' Dana said. 'Singular. I hope.'

She brushed the ant off and pulled up her trackies, giggling. 'Show's over.'

I realised Parko – our outdoor ed teacher – was right. She said we'd learn things about each other on this hike through the Magellan. It turns out Dana has been a professional model since she was twelve. I mean, that makes sense, but you wouldn't know unless she told you. It also turns out Dana and I wear the same black Bonds undies. Good to know.

She used a glove to sweep the ground then sat closer to Tariq. The fire became the centre of attention again. I could hear my tent calling.

'Did your nanna die?' Dana asked.

My mattress would have inflated itself by now. I can blow up my pillow in three big breaths. I wouldn't bother brushing my teeth. Again.

Boots shouldered me and broke the spell.

'Yep. Yes, my nanna survived. Bad Billy said he'd visit once he got out of hospital, but I doubted he would. And then, a few nights later, he was there waiting for me in my room when I got home from kindergarten. We played cars. He fell in love with the green VW Beetle that used to be my uncle's. We read books. Well, neither of us could read so we just looked at the pictures and made up stories. Bad Billy was an awesome storyteller. Mum said it would be okay for Billy to sleep over if it was okay with his parents.'

'That's sick,' Tariq said. 'You were five. He was twelve, man. He was after your body.'

Dana tutted.

'Should have gone for it, man. Did you go for it? All these years I've been telling everybody you're a virgin.'

It wasn't just sleep threatening to snuff out my story.

Boots sighed. 'All these years I've been telling everybody you're a cockhead, Tariq.'

'Yeah, Tariq, shut up,' Dana said. 'You cockhead.'

Tariq coughed into his hand. 'Gay.'

'Ignore him, Mason,' Dana said. 'Go on.'

'Billy slept on a mattress on the floor some nights. Other times he was happy with a blanket on the carpet. One night I asked him about his accident, and he told me he'd stood on a sausage.'

Tariq sucked air through his teeth. 'Deadly, those Bunnings snags.'

'His mate Jimmy died.'

'Billy and Jimmy?' Tariq said. 'Are you serious? Couldn't you make up some better names? How about Ahmed and Hassan for some diversity?'

'Died?' Dana asked. 'From the sausage?'

I nodded. 'Didn't make any sense to me. Didn't make any sense to Mum, either. In the beginning, anyway.'

'Can you remember what his sausage tasted like?' Tariq asked.

'In the beginning?' Chen said, as if Tariq hadn't opened his mouth.

'He was gone when I woke up and Mum always wanted to know what we talked about, so I told her Billy's stories. She recorded them on her phone. This went on for most of my kinder year. His last name was Templeton. He lived with his mum and dad and two older sisters on a farm down Gambon Road. His sisters were called Betty and Carmen. They gave him his nickname. He accidentally killed Carmen's pet rabbit. Dropped it into the water tank and couldn't reach it. He put yabbies from the dam in Betty's fish tank and they ate her goldfish. He melted the curtains in their lounge room playing with matches. Jimmy almost drowned when the raft they made sank in the middle of the dam. Neither of them could swim and they clung to the oil drum that kept the suction pipe off the bottom until Billy's dad heard them screaming and waded to their rescue. He said his dad belted them. Both. With his belt. On their wet legs. Made Jimmy bleed.'

'Savage,' Chen said.

'There aren't any farms on Gambon Road,' Tariq said. 'It's posh houses all the way to the army barracks. And Macca's. And KFC. And the leisure centre.'

'True,' I said.

'Full of shit,' Tariq grumbled. He locked his fingers behind his head.

'Did he go to jail?' Dana asked.

'Who?'

'Billy's dad. That's assault.'

'I don't know.'

'Jimmy wasn't even his own kid. You can't hit another person's kid,' Dana said.

'Shouldn't even hit your own kid,' Boots whispered. She hugged her knees.

'Did your mum report it?' Dana asked. 'You're supposed to. Mandatory reporting or something.'

I shook my head. 'That would have been awkward.'

'Awkward?' Dana said, eyes afire. 'Think of poor Jimmy.'

'Wait for it,' Boots said.

'Wait for what?' Dana asked.

'Mum couldn't see Billy,' I said. 'He was my imaginary friend.'

Tariq threw his hands in the air. 'Are you shitting me? You're worse than Chen.'

'He's not finished,' Boots said.

The fire cracked.

'Mum made notes. She went to the hospital and asked Terri the nurse if they had a record for Billy Templeton. They didn't, but Terri hooked Mum up with this woman from the historical society and she knew the story. It took her a few days, but she found an article from the *Tribune* about William Templeton and James Coad. James was killed instantly when the sausage of plastique explosive he'd been playing with blew up. His friend, William, lost both feet in the accident and died from his injuries at Nerrima hospital. Seventh of January. Nineteen forty-seven.'

'Fuck off,' Tariq said. He was leaning in now, hands on his lap.

'Goosebumps,' Chen said.

'Me too,' Dana said.

'They were playing at the rubbish tip and the explosives were old ordnance from the barracks.'

'You probably just overheard someone telling the story,' Tariq said.

'Maybe,' I said. 'But it gets weirder. His sister Carmen was still alive. She was eighty-nine at the time and living in a unit at Coolabah Village.'

'You *met* her?' Dana asked.

'Briefly,' I said. 'Mum introduced us and told her I was friends with her brother, asked if we could see a picture of Bad Billy and she slammed the door in our faces.'

'Savage,' Chen said again.

'Gee, I wonder why?' Dana said. She was hugging her knees now too.

'Mum kept looking,' I said. 'I think she got a bit obsessed. One night after kinder she shows me this black-and-white class photo ... Nerrima West Primary School, nineteen forty-six … and there he is. Billy. Right in the middle. At the back. I pointed him out and Mum's eyes started leaking.'

'You knew what he looked like?' Tariq said.

'Of course. He was my best friend.'

'How the hell did you know what he looked like?'

I showed him my palms.

'Is he here now?' Chen asked.

Tariq shot to his feet, scanning the bushes beyond the firelight.

'No,' I said. 'We found Jimmy's grave, me and Mum. Then we found Billy's grave. I gave him my uncle's toy VW. Put it next to his headstone. I never saw him again.'

'Huh!' Dana said. 'That's amazing.'

'It's like he needed to be seen,' Chen said. 'And once you'd seen him, he could leave.'

'I guess.'

'That's all anybody wants,' Boots said. 'Just to know they're not alone.'

I elbowed her and she nudged me back.

'Well, I need to piss,' Tariq said. 'And I'm looking for volunteers to help me remember I'm not alone while I'm doing it.'

YOUR MUM'S NIGHTIE

Stretch

In our song 'Party Machine', Phuong and I make up the backbone – groove and chords – until we get to the bridge section where he slips into this drunken 5/4 feel and I paint with a few plucked and sustained notes, bent all out of shape with the effects pedal. It's like the soundtrack for a dream sequence. A dream about rocking up to your English exam wearing your mum's nightie. The best sort of weird. The bridge-feel deserved a song of its own. Maybe the bridge-feel needed a *band* of its own.

'*Dana gives the best head,*' Marchie sang. '*But Candy's who I want in bed. She's a lean, mean party machine. Lean, mean party machine. There's no talk of love, just a clean rubber glove. Lean, mean party machine.*'

It was never a good song. Marchie's not quite the songwriter or frontman he likes to think he is. He always introduced it as our first hit single, but it wasn't a hit and we hadn't recorded it on anything except his phone. It was just our 'first'. We'd been playing it since we were all in Year 8. It was the song that brought us together as a band. The one we played first after the holidays to remind us what we were supposed to be doing. We'd been working on it for years and the more we worked on it, the more I fell out of love with it. It reminded me of Emily Taylor in that respect. When we'd first hooked up, on the Year 7 camp, I could have hand-painted the moon. So pretty and so, so smart, but the more I listened to her lyrics and moved to her groove, the more I wanted to hit 'shuffle'. Delete her from my playlist. Ditch her from my library. Never did, though. Never had the balls for that. If she hadn't told me about hooking up with that surfer dude while they were on holiday in Bali, we'd probably still be on repeat.

I'd never tell Marchie that Party Machine sucked, either, but it did. In thirteen different flavours. The whole 'woman as object' thing seemed boss when we were in Year 8 and living in fantasy porn land, but when your core fan base is mostly wide-eyed twelvies in oversized Nerrima High uniforms, it just sounds nasty. Not that it seemed to bother our fans. They'd hang around my amp like new moths, squeal and laugh at each other as they took turns to wig out. Do you hear what he's singing? Show a bit of dignity, please.

Then there's Pedro's special-needs bass line; just a single note – D – through all four chords in the verse and chorus, shifting to a C for the bridge and back to D again. Mind you, he still has to read it off the sheet. Never missed a note. Never raised a sweat. Never took a risk.

Daymo's keys feel like they're from another song, but they often do. Maybe he can't hear the rest of us or maybe he's just hell-bent on doing his own thing. He says the discord is deliberate, but the end result is like funeral music at a circus and that's not necessarily a bad thing.

The saving grace of the song is definitely the musical conversation I have with Phuong on the drums. The guy's a serious pro – unconsciously competent, as if the kit is some sort of weird appendage he's battled with since birth. He made peace with it some time back and recently auditioned for the College of the Arts in the city. That place only twinkles with the brightest of bright stars. To my knowledge, in the four years we've been playing together, he's never missed a beat. He can be marching-band tight and also swing it until you'd swear the rhythm's head's about to drop off. But it never does. One minute he's whispering jazz, the next he's all screamo and there's spit forming bubbles in the corners of his mouth.

So, we landed 'Party Machine' – perfectly on the four, like we'd never done before – and I felt something snap: not a string, but something more personal. A musical tendon.

A bone, perhaps. I had the strangest feeling that our band – All Day Wood – was over, and the sigh that made it through my lips sounded like relief. Like twenty-minutes-overdue-for-the-toilet sort of relief.

Before Marchie had even finished mumbling thanks to the twelvies through the microphone, the world picked up the tune in my head and began playing along.

Phuong got a message. 'Holy crap,' he said. 'Holy, holy crap.'

'What?' I asked.

'I'm in,' he said, straight-faced. 'I'm in.'

'Serious?' Daymo said. 'In where?'

'College of the Arts, bro,' Phuong said, and laid out a white-knuckled fill on the kit as a kind of musical exclamation mark. He tossed his sticks and leapt off his stool, whooping and punching the air.

I racked my guitar and hugged him – slapped his back and laughed until he drummed on mine.

'Brilliant, Phuong!' I bellowed. 'Absolutely brilliant, man.'

But the news wasn't music in everyone's ears.

'So that's it then?' Marchie said. 'That's the end of All Day Wood?'

'Nah,' Daymo said. 'We can get another drummer.'

Drummer, yes, I thought, but we'd never get another Phuong.

I should have said it. I should have grown a pair and told him that it *was* the end. Trouble is, I'm a guitarist, not a singer, and words feel awkward to me at times. Besides, why would I kill the thing if it's about to die a natural death anyway?

'What about that Year Ten guy?' Pedro asked. 'He's pretty good. His name's Ray, I think.'

'Do you know him?' Marchie asked, eyes suddenly aglow again.

'Sort of,' Pedro said.

One of the twelvies stepped closer to the stage. 'He's a she,' she said.

The others ignored her.

'Pardon?' I said.

'Ray, the drummer in Year Ten. She's my cousin.'

'True? Hear that, Marchie?'

'What?'

'Ray is . . . this girl's . . .'

'Meg,' she whispered.

'Ray is Meg's cousin.'

'Go and get him, Stretch. Let's have an audition.'

'Her,' Meg said.

'Ray's a chick?' Marchie said. 'Forget it.'

Meg stepped back, like Marchie had farted and I guess, in a way, he had.

'Forget it?'

'Yeah,' Marchie said. 'Chick drummers are useless.'

Phuong laughed, and crossed his arms.

'Not totally useless,' Marchie backtracked. 'Just no good for our line-up.'

With those words, I understood – with the conviction of experience – that music means totally different things to different people, even people in the same band. For Phuong, it represented a gift he wanted to hone. For Marchie, it was a vehicle to transport his planet-sized ego. For me, it was ... I didn't know what it was, but it wasn't either of those. We'd been going in different directions since the very beginning, but we'd been too busy being cool together to notice.

All Day Wood *had* to die.

'Sorry, Marchie, but my heart's not in it anymore.'

Did those words really come out of my mouth?

Marchie put his hands on his hips. 'What are you talking about, Stretch?'

'Four years, Marchie. We've been making the same noises, bungling the same songs. I'm tired. I want to try new stuff.'

'Fine,' he said. 'I've got some new songs I've been working on. A full album's worth. I'll let you work on some of those.'

I shook my head, mostly in disbelief. I knew Marchie well enough to know that 'an album's worth' of new material was probably a page of scribbled lines in his school diary. And it was stuff that, until now, he thought was too good for us.

It had to *die*.

'No thanks, I'm done.'

I didn't realise until that beat that the twelvies were staring at us with their mouths open. The big girl – Sarah – had tears in her eyes.

Meg opened her mouth to speak, then thought better of it.

'What?' I asked.

'Do you still want to meet my cousin?'

Marchie started shouting. Swearing. His face changed colour and he almost slammed the sliding door off its rollers as he left.

I crouched to Meg's eyeline. 'Yes please,' I said.

She took Sarah's hand and they jogged off into lunchtime.

Pedro rolled his eyes. 'That's a relief.'

'What?' I asked.

'Marchie.'

Daymo sighed. 'Oh, man, that's an understatement.'

'Are we good?' I asked.

In turn, the boys shrugged and nodded.

'Cheeseboard!' Phuong bawled, and counted us in for All Day Wood's one and only original instrumental piece.

Pedro was right. It was a relief, and I could hear it in every note we played.

Ray arrived mid-song. I'd seen her around, but she was hard to miss – leather wristbands, crazy piercings and pink punk pixie hair. Phuong called her over and told us to keep playing. She dropped onto his empty stool and didn't miss a beat.

Yeah, she had skills, all right. 'Cheeseboard' has a rockabilly feel and she played like she'd arranged it herself.

'Drum solo!' Phuong yelled, and we made some space for Ray.

She nailed it.

The twelvies were back and we wigged out with them when the song came crashing to an end.

The rest, they say, is history.

Marchie hooked up with a pub band and started raking in the cash after school.

I found out what music means to me. It's how I talk to my friends and the world when I get bored of words. I feel part of something bigger than me when I'm playing.

Skip forward to the final track, if you want to, if you're the sort of person who reads the liner notes of life, or if your middle name is Disney and you can't live without a happy ending.

The song is by an up-and-coming indie band called the Flaming Pom Poms.

It's an instrumental piece called 'Your Mum's Nightie'.

MAGELLAN

Tiff

We always went camping in the New Year. It was a family ritual. My mother – a dentist in Nerrima – had a disturbing 'back to nature' side that my father – a regional manager for Woolworths – encouraged at every opportunity. Add my spineless older brother to the mix and you can see the problems with democracy. There's the ambitious one (Mother), the enabler (Father) and the mindless masses (Sean). All I'm trying to say is that I know what it's like to feel invisible.

'Let's go hiking. Magellan Peninsula,' Mum said.

'Sounds great,' said Dad. 'What do you reckon, Sean?'

'Yeah. Cool. Whatever.'

'Tiff?'

'It doesn't matter what I think. Why do you even ask?' Mum stroked a strand of hair behind my ear.

I turned away.

'Don't be like that, Tiff,' she said. 'Of course it matters what you think.'

'Fine,' I said. 'I'd rather go to Aqualand.'

Sean was the only one who sniggered aloud, but Mum and Dad were laughing on the inside.

Mum grabbed my fingers. 'We've had this discussion, love.'

'Every year since we went,' Sean said. '*Seven* years ago.'

'Yess,' I hissed, 'and still you ignore me.'

'We're not ignoring you, Tiff,' Dad said. 'Even if we forget about the kids who bullied Sean ...'

'And the fight,' Sean interrupted.

'And the fight,' Dad said.

'And the stitches,' Sean said.

Dad held up his hand. 'Even if we forget about the bad stuff that happened at the park but had *nothing* to do with the park itself, Aqualand was an epic, epic failure.'

'Especially for me,' I said.

'We didn't know there were height restrictions,' Mum said.

'Yeah, that was your fault, Tiff,' Sean said. 'For being such a short-arse seven-year-old.'

Mum shut him down with a pointer finger aimed between his eyes, but she couldn't hide her smile.

I stormed out. It wasn't much of a storm – just a few frustrated gusts of wind from my nose and some drizzle from my eyes – but I *did* storm.

Skip forward to January and that storm was still blowing. We were on Uncle Jim's boat, the *Enterprise II*, sailing for the wild end of the Magellan Peninsula, just as our Great Leader said we would. My lips were bitter with vomit. Mum had given up patting my back. She'd left me gripping the rail to take her turn steering. Every time Sean made eye contact, he pretended to gag and it wasn't helping.

Uncle Jim sat upwind of me and hung his bare feet over the side.

'This is Point Smythe,' he explained, nodding to the headland in front of us. 'The peninsula is on the other side. Have you guys been walking there before?'

I shook my head, gripped the rail. I shouldn't have shaken my head.

Uncle Jim raised his eyebrows above the rims of his Oakleys. 'You okay?'

'How long to go?'

'Half an hour or so. Going to make it?'

I offered a shrug.

He patted my bare knee. 'This will pass, Tiff. Soon as you hit the beach, you'll feel better, I promise. You will love the Magellan. It's another world. Another *world*.'

And, as we rounded the point and Magellan Peninsula came into view, I had another little chuck and spit to celebrate.

Bald-man mountains sat on their haunches. Their scruffy forest cloaks fell away to reveal white scars of beaches. Here and there warty grey rocks poked through the greenery or waded into the ocean. I couldn't see a house, a track, or a person anywhere in that panorama.

This place was the exact opposite of Aqualand.

We anchored beside a beach so bright it would have been visible from space and Sean pretended to vomit on me. Mum held her mouth and patted his back. Dad gave me a hand up.

We loaded the zodiac – four hiking packs and five people – and hung on for our lives as Uncle Jim ran the little boat right up onto that sugar sand.

Back on dry land, my guts finally stopped trying to climb out of my mouth.

We took it in turns to hug Uncle Jim and I got a wet boot helping launch the dinghy. As the whining motor propelled him back out to the yacht, I nearly started crying.

Don't leave me here.

But the feeling passed. The little waves sounded like applause and the shadowy jungle echoed with birdsong. The place even smelled like adventure.

Packs on, straps tight.

'Right,' Sean said. 'Which way do we go?'

'Which way do *you* think we should go?' Mum said.

Sean moaned. 'Oh, not this crap again. Can't you just say?'

Dad pinched my elbow and quickly pointed along the beach. A small bright orange triangle sat above the high tide line a kilometre or so away.

'How about we check out that marker?' I suggested.

Mum and Dad grinned.

Sean started jogging.

My backpack is called 'Intrepid'. I like that word and I remembered how much I liked my pack before we'd made it to that first marker. It feels like part of me and has everything I need for four whole days – food, clothes, my half of the tent I share with my brother, and chocolate. The pack never seemed as heavy as my schoolbag, even with the chocolate.

The track behind the orange marker led us off the beach into the cool forest. It followed the line of the bay for a while, then began snaking up a rise that quickly became a hill, that eventually turned into a full-blown mountain. Mount Fitzpatrick. I didn't like my pack quite as much by the time we'd made it to the viewing platform at the peak, but I did like the view. We could see the beach where we'd started, Point Smythe across the water and that hard-ruled line of the horizon.

And we could see lunch.

'We should camp here,' Sean said through a mouthful.

Dad dropped lettuce from his wrap onto the map unfolded on his thighs. He flicked the lettuce. 'We're not quite halfway to the official campsite.'

'Serious?' Sean said, and hung his head.

'Mostly downhill, though.'

I followed the line he traced with his finger on the map to the place he tapped. Another beach. Limecutters Bay.

Mostly we walked together. Sean went first on the narrow sections, until he saw a snake. Like an old black-and-white comedy, he backed into Dad who backed into Mum who knocked me on my bum. We pulled ourselves together and the snake was still there. Right in the middle of the track.

'It's got something in its mouth,' Mum whispered.

'Frog,' Dad said.

We watched the snake eat the frog. Totally gross and totally fascinating. The frog was bigger than the snake's head, but its jaws unhinged, stretched, and eventually all we could see were legs. I didn't breathe normally until the snake poured off the track glossing like used oil.

I watched where I put every step after that. Mostly so I wouldn't stand on a snake, but then I forgot about the snakes and I was watching my boots because I was walking on a rough track and that's just what you do. And then I forgot about my boots as we slid over stumps, ducked under ferns and pressed through gaps between boulders. I was too busy being *intrepid.*

We saw dolphins in the bay, sea eagles fighting (or flirting) in mid-air, and an enormous flock of dark-feathered seabirds feeding on an even bigger and darker school of fish. My shoulders got sore. My feet ached. We just kept walking. All the way to Limecutters Bay.

We set up the tents. Dad and Sean lay down for a rest, but I was buzzing. Mum shushed me with a finger to her lips and then, using hand signals, suggested we walk to the beach. We raced the last fifty metres. Mum kept running straight into the waves, fully clothed. I followed her in, roaring at the cold and the madness. We thrashed through the lazy surf until we were waist deep and puffing.

'Now I need to pee,' I said.

Mum squatted and, eventually, sighed. 'I don't.'

Eating pasta by the light of our torches that night, I realised the storm in my head had passed. I loved everyone and everything. I loved my family – even my whiny brother made me laugh when he dropped spaghetti on the back of his hand and started crying like he was two. I loved the sky and the smell of the dirt and the breeze making the trees above us sigh and our tent flap and I loved the night-birds calling. And chocolate.

I didn't stay awake for long, just long enough to work out that this camp, this trip, was glue. Superglue. The stuff that held our family together.

Every day we ate our packs lighter and the Magellan kept giving – rainbows, sunsets and shooting stars.

On the third night, Mum and I were secretly sharing the last of her chocolate at the beach. We watched the blood moon rise, full and red over the ocean.

'In all my years,' Mum whispered, 'I've never seen a moonrise as beautiful as that.'

I found her hand like I was five again. 'Thanks.'

'What for?'

'For everything. For the chocolate. For this trip. For being intrepid. For the moonrise.'

She breathed a laugh. 'You're welcome.'

And then she died.

She made a sound like she'd remembered something, then slumped to the sand as though someone had cut all her strings.

I still had her hand.

A blood vessel had burst in her brain. Cerebral aneurism. For a long time after that Dad, Sean and I watched our every step. I'd lose myself in something and forget for just a minute, then I'd remember and feel sick. Sick because, for a minute, I'd forgotten her, then sick because I remembered she was gone. Sick of the hollow sounds my heart made.

We were still bruised and sore when the next New Year came around, but we rallied. When it came time to choose a destination for our holiday, Aqualand didn't get a look-in. Sean suggested we head back to the Magellan, but Dad and I weren't ready for that. In the end, it was my suggestion that won the vote.

'Whose crazy idea was this?' Dad bawled. His diving mask was crooked, and his voice sounded nasal and cartoon.

Sean gripped my arm. I don't think he was even aware he was doing it.

They lowered our cage into the black-blue ocean and my heart was beating strong. Badum badum badum. The shadows. The black disc of an eye peering between the bars. All those teeth.

I didn't forget her. I never will. She's there in my eyes when I look in the mirror. I hear her in my words sometimes. She's always with me.

Especially when I'm being intrepid.

Like when we're diving with great whites.

'Yeahhh!' I roared into my snorkel.

THINGLESS

Ranen

I totally get why you want that fast car and that big new house and the TV that is so massive and bright that birds fly into it when you watch nature documentaries. I understand the appeal of your beautiful dream boyfriend or dream girlfriend or gender-free dream and your jetski and swimming pool to ride it around in and your helipad beside your motorbike track at your other beach mansion.

You want to be so hot that people melt when they look at you and yet you want to be so cool that when you enter a party people want your ice in their drink. And hot cool people have lots of sexy sex and friends with benefits and job offers that smell like bacon cooking. When you google your own name, the autofill suggests adding 'nude'. Your bank will beg you for mercy under the weight of your enormous accounts. Even doors that aren't automatic will open for you automatically. Gymnasiums will want you to breathe inside them, share your perspiration, maybe fondle a light switch and use the amenities. There's a strong market for your sweaty gym towels on eBay so, for you, staying buff is a kind of community service. You have a diamond finger for every ring.

I understand the appeal.

They get at you when you're little and they culture this culture of Things, so when you get old enough to want, you know the things you're supposed to want for. You know the stuff to stuff your stuff with.

They've tricked you. They've sucked you in, but it wasn't really hard. Stuff is so pretty and it's hard to say no. Why would you? I could tell you a thousand reasons to say no to stuff, but you wouldn't believe me.

Here, I'll *show* you ...

Look around you. I mean *really* look. Find a window if you're inside; better still, find a door or two, take yourself outside and find the horizon in every direction. Look at the sky and the ground at your feet. Take note of the clouds and the stars, the cool trees and the hard concrete, for this is my home. My world. All of it. Every blinking heavenly body and cigarette butt. Every upturned shopping trolley and crystal stream. Every plant pushing through the cracks and every peppery sand dune. The soft railway siding weeds and the rainbow oil-slick puddles.

I am of this world. Teenage vagabond.

Every day is a school day and everyone I meet is my teacher. My classroom is the surf beach, the bus stop, that cool tree. I know what I know because I listened to what they said. I asked questions when there were questions to be asked and I listened to the answers. I tried opinions on like hats and left many by the side of the road. They fed me and clothed me with the things they left behind. Thanks for that. Cats taught me how to find a warm spot, dogs taught me how to play.

I'm not very wise, but I know how to play the game. I know where the public toilets are, and that cleanliness is next to invisibility on the social spectrum. I know that in the pressure cooker of daily life, a kindness given is a kindness given, a smile is a precious commodity and helping café staff put chairs out in the morning can taste like sweet coffee.

I'm not homeless.

Homeless suggests that I want for a home, but the world is my home.

I'm thingless.

Well, not completely thingless – wearing fig leaves is frowned upon in this Garden of Eden. I have a blanket and a coat, odd socks and an even odder hat. I have a toothbrush and a library card and if I run out of toothpaste, I know how to get more – my opening line is 'Is there any way I can help you?'

I have a bag for all my things that I can carry with one finger and if I lost it tomorrow, I might get wet or I might get cold or I might go hungry for a while. Have you ever been cold or wet or hungry? I guess another way to ask that might be, 'Have you ever looked forward to eating, had a shower or put your jacket back on again?' Every other animal on the planet can cope with that from time to time but we poor hairless apes can't.

That's why we need Things.

If we get cold, hungry and wet, we can *die*.

That's why we need a roof over our heads and four remote controls.

That's why we need refrigerators big enough to park a car in and reverse-cycle air conditioners that make the streetlights dim when they turn themselves on.

Comfy? Of course you're comfortable. Discomfort is *death*.

Maybe you've forgotten how to sleep on a blanket of leaves. Maybe you've forgotten the magic of waking with dew in your hair under a throw rug of stars. Have you even heard the birds' pillow talk as the shadows are washed away? The night-shift owls are calling, 'Good day to you, sir.' The day-shift magpies whisper, 'Are you awake?'

Yes, I'm awake.

More awake than I've ever been.

You're missing out, my sisters, my brothers. My others.

It's a new day.

A *new* day.

Don't go to school today: come with me and learn the world. We'll count the waves and read the stories in the clouds. We'll fill ourselves with the smell of the saltbush and draw in the sand with our toes. We'll help where we can and make friends from all over the world. Old ones and young ones, fur and feather. Our brains will grow bigger and our hearts will grow warmer until we forget what Things are for.

GRASS

Cassie

I

I knew.

Some part of me knew I was pregnant as Mum was leaving. I knew, but it didn't matter that she was leaving. Some part of me was glad she was going. So long as she kept paying her share of the rent from Belgium, I'd be fine. Better than fine.

I'd be free.

Free to leave my towel on the floor and my dishes in the sink. Free to bounce any boy I fancied, in the kitchen if I wanted. On top of the dishes in the sink. Yeah, that'd be hot. And just a little bit dirty.

At least I couldn't get pregnant.

Two months later and he was still my little secret. A few boys came knocking. One of them – a huge Islander called Possum – made the kitchen table crack in his enthusiasm, but my little man had bolted the door. I did eventually piss on a stick, but it wasn't news to me. I knew he was a boy the same way I knew I was pregnant, like I'd remembered.

Nev didn't notice. If anyone was going to, it'd be him. Didn't take his eyes off me from the moment I arrived at work to the minute he dropped me off. Crusty old prick.

His words were always business – 'Mrs Davidson in Bellamy Street said you did a lovely job of the front yard. Said you missed a few spots in the back.' – but his glasses fogged up and his lips were wet. He was a perve, but he paid in cash and June – his wife – would tear him a new one with her bare hands if he tried anything. In a way he was part of my ticket to freedom. He gave me a job when I left Nerrima High. Maybe school left me. Okay, it was a mutual decision and Nev gave me work. I became his permanent part-time boobs to watch and if I decided to whipper-snip *around* the massive dog turds in Mrs Davidson's backyard in Bellamy, he'd mention it and I'd flash him a smile.

'Yeah, sorry about that, Nev. I was avoiding the Freckles of Death.'

And he'd laugh harder and louder than any grown man

should at the thought of me spotted with weed-whacked dog shit.

→

He'd work it out eventually. Everybody would. Ain't nowhere to hide a pumpkin on a rake. There are probably parts of the world where sixteen is considered young to have a baby, but Clarendon isn't one of them. In The Don we don't care what you think. My friends, the Tuvalu sisters – Islander twins from around in Minti Drive – had their babies two days apart. They were fourteen at the time. Like Mum, you could say that their lives were ruined, but when you see them pushing their four-year-olds on the swings in the dusty park, they don't look broken.

Some of us just want a kid.

Monique, the Sudanese girl three doors down, thought that condoms were for bananas. She has two kids now – with the same dad. Akembe might have been an accident, but her brother wasn't.

Some of us just want a family.

I stopped smoking tobacco the day Mum left. When that second pink line magically appeared on the piss stick, I stopped drinking, too. The boys I hung out with were good at faking sober when the cops or their mums were around. I got good at faking drunk. Unlike every other teenager's Coke bottle in The Don, mine actually contained Coke.

Dope was another story. There are only so many times you can refuse a toke before your friends start asking about your health. Besides, the nights never seemed as dark when I was rubber-headed.

Emilio liked a choof. He was twenty. The coffee-coloured skin on his arms had been blued with tattoos. He always had a roll of cash and a pouch of hydro. He always had a smile for me and some goss to share. A couple of cones in on a private session and he'd just want to talk. And talk. He was a mechanic and he understood the way The Don worked. He'd been tinkering under her bonnet since he was little. Told me his boss made most of his money from a hydro set-up behind his workshop. Three cones later his words would dry up and he'd just want to kiss in slow motion. My jaw, my neck, my chest would be crimson with beard rash until the next morning.

Emilio was the first one to notice.

He'd made me howl like a wolf before breakfast and now his head was on my thigh, his hand on my belly – a woodworker stroking his creation – and he froze. The woodworker turned cold-handed doctor, prodding and squeezing until I had to roll away. He bounced across the bed and stared at me, squinting to read my face in the gloom.

'When are you due?'

'I have to go to work.'

➳

I'm sure it was just a coincidence, but Mum chose that day to phone. First time since she'd left. I couldn't get a word in. She spoke with an accent; one she'd had in her handbag since I was born. One she took out for new men and drunken parties.

'Listen, love,' she said.

Did I have any other choice?

'I will not be able to ... how do you say this? I will not be able to pay the rent this month.'

'Rent' came out 'runt' and I laughed into the mouthpiece.

'This is costing a fortune. I have to go, ma chérie,' she said. 'I hope you – '

I hung up before she did.

She sounded like Gran, and later that afternoon as I stood in the baby food aisle at the supermarket, I realised she *was* Gran.

Gran left when Mum was sixteen. She moved to Maybeline, developed an accent and died of lung cancer.

Nev dropped me home. Emilio's Falcon sat in the drive. Emilio sat on the step, smoking. Smoking and smiling. It wasn't a sleazy smile or a hungry smile, it was a smile like one of the twins' kids in the glow of an iPad – more eyes than mouth. He didn't say anything, just watched me.

He must have done the maths. He must have known the kid wasn't his, yet here he was. He butted his cigarette on the concrete, stood and took the bags of groceries from me, kissed my cheek.

That kiss. I wish I'd gone to a surgeon straight away and had that kiss cut out. Would have saved us both a lot of pain. That kiss festered into him wanting to hold my hand as we watched TV.

It bled into the bedroom.

'Are you okay? Comfortable?'

'Fine,' I said, but I wasn't.

A few weeks later he moved in and paid his share of the rent from the cashbox he hid on top of the cupboard. He shook Nev's hand when he dropped me at work.

'I love you,' he said, one bent Saturday night.

I kissed his eyelids and smiled.

I only loved one thing.

And that one thing kept growing.

II

I told Nev.

'That's ... fantastic news. I'm so ... happy for you. And Emilio.'

But his face didn't match his words. His face said he'd failed.

I took his hand and kissed his grassy knuckles. 'Thanks, Nev.'

Then our words got all business again and I told him I'd work until the baby dropped.

We both knew I didn't really have a choice, but we pretended like I did.

➳

At the start of my third trimester, choices began to arrive out of the tyre-smoky air of The Don. Hard choices.

Emilio introduced me to his boss, Spider. We played it cool, but Spider eyed my belly and did the maths. He smiled.

In my head, I'd never planned to get pregnant, but my body had other ideas.

Spider was made of iron and earth and smelled like bourbon on old leather. I'd never want to share a house with him but sharing a house and sharing a bed are different things.

He was the moonlight that had made me flower.

He held my throat when we did it. It looked sexy in the movies. There was nothing sexy about it. Nothing.

'What's she doing here?' Spider asked.

'She's with me.'

I stared at the floor.

'Yeah, well, we've got business,' he said.

Emilio shifted feet. He pressed the car keys into my palm.

⤞

Everybody knew where Spider lived. He didn't have a lawn to mow, just dead Subarus. His porch light blazed day and night like he was too stupid or paranoid to turn it off. Nobody knew his real name. Maybe Spider was his real name? Not the strangest name in The Don.

It suited him. If he was in the room, you'd want to keep half an eye on him. His neck and his hands were tattooed with a crazy mix of tribal swirls, playing cards and black-eyed skulls, but the skin beneath his collared business shirt was hairless, pale and free of ink. The tattoos and the heavy silver jewellery on his fingers and his face were his camouflage, made him look tougher than he really was. They took the attention away from his eyes that were way too big, way too blue and way too innocent for a player like Spider.

I hoped the kid would have his eyes.

The sun went down and I'd almost fallen asleep – hand on my kicking and squirming belly – when Emilio tore the car door open.

His teeth were bared. 'Keys!'

I threw them. He fumbled the catch and swore.

'What is it? What happened?'

'Shut up. Hang on.'

The seatbelt grabbed before I could click it home. Screaming tyres, howling engine. I held the dash and the doorhandle. Country road speeds around the narrow streets of The Don. Must have been doing eighty when we hit the speed bump at the end of Bellamy Street. I bounced hard off the roof, bit my tongue.

'Slow down!' I squealed, but it didn't get through his bubble of fear or rage or whatever it was. 'The baby!'

He slammed the brakes and my face smacked the dash. I ended on my knees in the footwell. I tasted blood.

'Get out,' Emilio growled. 'Quickly. Go!'

More than a little punch-drunk, I didn't react straight away.

'Get out. Getout. GetOUT. GETOUT!'

I fumbled with the handle and dropped to my side on the weedy nature strip. Emilio didn't wait for me to close the door. The tyre smoke clawed at my throat and I spat.

'You okay, love?' It was a man's voice, deep and accented.

I wiped my face with the back of my hand. The prick of light from a phone torch blinded me.

'You're bleeding,' the voice said. 'Here, sit.'

Warm fingers closed on my arm and eased me upright.

'Here,' he said, and handed me an ironed handkerchief.

I took it, mopped at my nose and lips. It had been months since I'd seen my own blood. It was comforting, somehow.

'Thank you.'

'No problem. Are you okay? Is the baby okay?'

I felt the round of my belly through my singlet.

'I'm fine. We're fine. Thanks.'

'Can you stand? Let me help you.'

I didn't need the help, but I leaned into him anyway. He smelled of faded cologne.

'Do you need me to call someone?'

I recognised my surroundings. I knew the man.

'It's Mr Tuvalu, isn't it?'

'Yes. Peter. That's me. Have we met?'

'Sort of. I know your twins. I'm Cassie.'

'Cassie? Cassie Barker? So it is! Will you come inside? For a drink?'

'I . . .'

'I insist. Loti will help you clean up properly. I don't feel comfortable leaving you like this.'

His hand cupped my elbow and guided me along the road and up the stairs. The door opened with a breath of strange cooking smells. Kids in pyjamas barged past me and attached themselves to Peter's legs. He carried them – one in each arm – into the crowded kitchen.

The twins and their boyfriends huddled with their backs to me on one side of a table that would seat four in a cafe. The twins' mother, Loti, stirred a pot at the stove and kissed her husband without missing a beat. He mumbled in her ear and our eyes met. She dropped her spoon, killed the gas and wiped her hands.

'My poor darling! Cassie! Cassie!' she said and hugged my head.

The kitchen fell quiet. Everybody stared.

'Are you okay?' Loti asked. 'Let me look at you.'

She ushered me into the bathroom and closed the door behind us. She took Peter's handkerchief, wet it at the sink and dabbed my face like I was two years old. It didn't really hurt, but tears welled and fell. Loti mopped them up without saying a thing. When the blood had stopped flowing and the tears had stopped flowing, she held her palm above my belly.

'May I?'

'Of course,' I said, and sniffed.

The little show pony in there started kickboxing as soon as Loti's hand touched my singlet.

Her whole face lit up. 'So strong,' she said. 'How can you sleep at night?'

It was a simple question, an innocent question, but it opened the keg of tears again and Loti held me like nobody ever had. In the first second, I felt relief; the second, I felt hope; and the third, I felt shame. I broke her hug to wipe my face.

Loti held my shoulders. 'Eat with us.'

'I . . .'

'You have to eat.'

➳

We held hands around the table to say grace and the meal – rice and . . . something – was a feast of elbows and stories. After all the noodles I'd eaten in front of the TV – with Mum and lately with Emilio – dinner at the Tuvalus' felt ancient. Tribal. Every bite I swallowed made my bones warmer.

Peter insisted on walking me home, but not before I'd been washed by a waterfall of hugs. The twins, their children, their boys. Everybody.

Loti kissed my cheek.

'You are always welcome here, Cassie. Day or night.'

And as Peter's departing footsteps rang heavy on the stairs of the unit, I locked the steel security screen and put the door on the chain. The quiet that crowded in made me turn on the TV and every light in the house.

It was after 10 pm when someone knocking on the wall set my heart off.

I froze behind the door. Had I imagined it?

They rapped again, heavier this time.

'Who is it?' I shouted.

'It's me,' Spider said.

'What do you want?'

'Can I come in?'

'What do you want?'

'I've got something for you. For the kid.'

I opened the door on the chain. He leaned against the railing with a thick roll of notes pinched between his greasy fingers.

'I don't want your money.'

'Don't be like that, Cass. It's my kid too.'

'It's not your kid.'

He raised his chin, smiled. 'We'd better get a DNA test, just in case.'

'He's not your kid.'

'He? It's a boy?'

'Fuck off.'

'Cass, be reasonable. I'm trying to help out here. Trying to take responsibility.'

Spider leapt off the railing and crashed into the security screen, but I'd seen him coming. I didn't blink.

He laughed, but it came out as a nervous chuckle.

'Hope you've got a good lawyer.'

I closed the door in his face, which set off an attack on the security screen that lasted a good ten seconds. I stood there, holding the one breath, until his boots set the concrete steps ringing again. I sighed, but there wasn't much relief in it.

III

Emilio never came back. I washed and dried his clothes and packed them on top of the tools in his workbag. I didn't know what to do with them, so I left the lot in the corner of the room. I took his cashbox down from the top of the cupboard and counted nearly four thousand dollars onto the bed. I put the money back in the box and the box in his bag. The zip sounded final.

»—►

The last three weeks of my pregnancy waddled by like a pensioner in a walking frame. Nev's June called or sent a text a couple of times a day over the weekends and Nev wouldn't let me lift a thing. I wanted to lift stuff. I wanted to strain. I wanted to bounce on a trampoline or something. No offence to the little dude, but I wanted my body back.

I ate with the Tuvalus on Thursday nights and I didn't see or hear from Spider again.

Not until it all came tumbling down.

»—►

'I have to pick up the ride-on, then I think we'll call it a day,' Nev said.

It was only two o'clock, but it was steamy. The poor man. I'd taken to wearing T-shirts and bought myself a maternity bra as my boobs had grown, but I couldn't hide them anymore.

Nev needed a maternity bra for his eyes.

'You're the boss,' I said.

He didn't drive to Benson's, right in the middle of town, where he normally had the mower serviced, but instead picked through the industrial estate down the rough end of Clarendon. Down past the disused car yards piled high with rusty scrap steel. Down past the bent mesh fences lined with wind-blown rubbish. Over the oily creek, beside the graffiti-coloured freight cars of the railway siding into the driveway of Davis Automotive.

Davis Automotive? That was the place where Emilio used to work. That was the place ...

'You can wait here, if you like,' Nev said to my boobs. 'Do you want me to leave the aircon on?'

I nodded, sank down in my seat and pulled my cap over my eyes.

Nev chuckled. 'No nodding off,' he said. 'I won't be long.'

The workshop was open to the street and I could see three – no, four – mechanics going about their business. None of them were Emilio. None of them were Spider. The walls were covered in faded posters – cars and women in bikinis draped over cars – and at the very back of the workshop a gap in the benches allowed access to a narrow steel door that carried two heavy pad bolts and locks to suit. Locked tight. In the middle of the day.

Nev came out of the office folding a receipt, Spider hot on his heels.

I locked my door and slunk down as far as my belly would let me. I pretended to sleep.

The trailer ramps clanged to the driveway and I recognised the sound of Nev's ride-on starting. The ute rocked as the mower was driven aboard. Nev's door opened and I held my breath.

'Thanks for all that, Martin,' Nev said. 'Very happy with your service. I'll be back.'

'No problems. Thanks.'

The ute revved and I breathed again, but too soon.

Fingernails rapped on my window and I looked up, startled.

Spider grinned in at me, bent and straightened his tattooed fingers in a creepy wave.

'See you tonight,' he mouthed.

I stared.

'Okay,' Nev said. 'Drop you at home, Cass?'

'Thought I might go to Central.'

'Shopping? Again? You went shopping last night.'

I shrugged. 'I'm building a nest.'

Nev laughed harder than he should have. 'Right you are then.'

➳

Truth was I'd finished my nest-building nearly a month before. I'd bought an Ikea cot. I borrowed Nev's battery drill and put it together in ten minutes. All of the baby clothes, the pusher and the plastic bath were from the twins. I'd finished my nest-building, but that night I needed the lights, the easy listening and the food court.

To begin with, I thought my butter-chicken dinner wasn't sitting right but the cramping developed a rhythm and by closing time it had dawned on me that my little Vegemite was on his way. The baby was coming. I thought about walking home, but at the automatic doors I had a contraction that bent me over. I made a noise that was anything but easy listening.

A Chinese girl in school uniform asked if I was okay. I nodded, through the white pain, but she was unconvinced.

'Should I call someone for you? An ambulance?'

By then the pain had started to subside.

'No. No, thank you. I'm okay.'

But her hand was on my shoulder. 'Can I walk you to your car?'

'I don't have a car.'

'Wait here, I'll get a taxi.'

'I just . . . I'll be . . .'

She jogged to the edge of the road and shattered the hum of the shopping centre with a shrill whistle. I'd managed to straighten up by the time she returned.

'He's coming,' she said. 'There's a taxi coming. Won't be long.'

'Thanks,' I said.

She held my arm all the way to the roadside. I could have made it under my own steam but by then I didn't want to.

At sight of me the taxi driver – a young Sikh man wearing a blue turban – hurried around to open my door.

'Hospital?' he asked.

'No, I'm okay,' I said. 'Clarendon. Thank you.'

And I *was* okay. Better than okay. The cramping faded and left in its wake a kind of drug buzz. I heard the driver talking, but my canoe was floating on some crazy calm water.

He's coming. My boy is coming.

I wish I'd realised that my canoe had to go over Niagara Falls first.

»—▷

I paid the driver.

'Would you like me to wait? I can take you to the hospital.'

I only had to grab my bag. I'd been packed for a month. Little punk wasn't due for another four days. They'd probably send me home again.

'Okay. Thanks.'

Toothbrush. Phone charger. Should I leave the porch light on? No – it says I'm not home if I leave it on during the day. Maybe I should leave it on – it's like a beacon of hope at night. No – off saves electricity. Yes – I finally decided. I needed the hope.

Spider stood on the verandah, arms crossed, mouth open in a forced smile.

I hadn't locked the security door. I was only going to be a minute.

'What do you want?' I asked.

He flashed his palms. 'A talk. That's all.'

'So talk,' I said. 'Make it quick. My taxi's waiting.'

'We've got plenty of time,' he said, gesturing at the empty street. The taxi had gone.

'I told the towelhead that I'm the dad-to-be. I made it home in time. Told him that we didn't need him anymore.'

He snatched open the security screen before I had a chance to lock it.

I slammed the door in his face, deadlocked it and hooked the chain home. A barrage of fist blows and steel-toed kicks threatened to peel it off its hinges.

I covered my ears.

In the fight between Spider and the door, the door eventually won.

I uncovered my ears.

'I just want to talk,' he fumed.

'So talk!'

This time, when Spider hit the door, it must have been shoulder first. The frame cracked. The whole flat shuddered. He hit it again. And again.

The door won round two as well, but not by much.

I dialled the police but didn't connect the call. Spider and his rage would have battered the door down long before they got here.

I phoned the Tuvalus instead. One of the twins answered.

'It's Cassie,' I said. 'I need . . .'

'Cassie?'

The next contraction mowed me down. There was no rising wave of pain, it came on like a leg cramp but in my guts. I fell to my knees. I dropped the phone.

'Cassie?'

The pain escaped as a bellow. I sounded like a dying cow but there was nothing I could do.

'Cassie?' the thin voice from the phone said again. 'What's the matter? Are you okay?'

I couldn't answer. Couldn't breathe.

'Open the fucking door!' Spider roared and launched himself into another assault.

At the height of the pain, on my hands and knees, something gave way and the heat of it filled my shorts and ran down my legs. I thought I'd pissed myself, but the relief, when it came, was different.

Spider snarled and swore in frustration, then everything went quiet.

My senses returned and I breathed again. The phone hissed with empty static and when I called again, I got the user-busy signal.

I phoned an ambulance.

A musical explosion of breaking glass erupted from the lounge. A garden rock the size of a loaf of bread tumbled onto the carpet. Spider had given up on the door and the window offered little resistance.

A new wave of dread closed around my throat, but the slope of the block meant the smashed front window was well above head height. I watched, panting, through the thin curtain as the shadow of Spider ran hard across the lawn and leapt for the sill. His tattooed fingers closed on the only part of the frame that wasn't sharp with teeth of glass and he hung there. I wrapped a pointy piece of broken window in the hem of my T-shirt and ripped the curtain aside.

Our eyes met.

'Let me in,' he growled.

'No.'

'We have to talk.'

'No. Fuck off.'

'That baby is mine.'

I stabbed his hand. He swore and let go, landed awkwardly and tumbled onto the path. In a second he was on his feet again. He stared, teeth exposed, then scanned the yard. He slunk into the shadows and returned – rumbling – with the neighbour's wheelie bin. He arranged it beneath the window and climbed on top.

I waved my spike of glass at his face.

'Let me in.'

His eyes weren't right. He was psycho. Horror-movie psycho.

I dropped my weapon and ran. More glass shattered and I knew he was clearing a way in.

There was nowhere to hide. I grabbed my bag. I unlocked the front door and the moment his boots thudded to the carpet, I stepped onto the porch, deadlocking the door behind me.

'Fuuuck!'

I toppled the wheelie bin and wide-legged it for the road. I could hear sirens, but they seemed way off. I heard Spider land on the rubbish, and I ran, as fast as my belly would let me, for Mrs Tio's porch light. We'd hated each other since I was in primary school, but she had a Jesus on the cross beside her doorbell.

I didn't make it.

My world turned all slow-motion as another contraction bloomed its petals of pain from deep inside. On my grazed knees, in the middle of the road, I heard the footfalls.

I felt the hand on my back.

Warm hand. Gentle hand. Loti Tuvalu's hand.

'Cassie, my poor darling. Are you okay? The ambulance is coming, my sweet. Won't be long.'

IV

Having a baby hurts like hell. What a surprise! I'd planned on being a tough chick, but I was bawling my eyes out before we made it to the hospital. Seven hours later I was a puddle of sweat and snot and tears and blood, but it was worth it. Every minute. Every second.

Six pounds and seven ounces. Nearly three kilograms. I called him Darcy after a kid I knew at school. I didn't really like the kid, but I loved his name. Ten fingers and ten toes, he had more hair on his back than he did on his head. The nurse said the head hair would grow, but I didn't care.

The whole Tuvalu mob visited. They brought flowers and I cried. The kids wanted to hold Darcy, but their mothers wouldn't let them, so they patted his head instead and I cried some more.

So much for tough chick.

When Darcy was two days old and we were still in hospital, the cops came.

The nurse had taken Darcy so I could have a shower and the cops came and suddenly my head was screaming, and I knew they'd come to take him away. We should've left the hospital as soon as I could walk. Me and Darcy should've snuck out in the middle of the night. Now the cops were here, and it was too late. My hands made fists and I eyed the guns in their holsters. They introduced themselves – as nice as pie – but I wasn't listening. I was planning my escape. I thought I could take out the guy with a well-placed kick but not in the balls – he didn't look like he had any. The woman, on the other hand, looked like a roller-derby champion.

'If you'll excuse me for a minute,' I said, all ladylike. 'I have to check on . . .'

'We won't keep you long,' roller-derby said, stepping aside.

It's a trap. They want me to make a break so they can . . .

'Do you live at unit one, twenty-seven Hawkers Road, Clarendon?' the woman asked.

'Yes.'

'There was a fire there last night,' the man said. 'The brigade managed to contain the damage to the front room and the kitchen.'

I sat on my bed. Stupid paranoid bitch. They weren't here to lock me up. They weren't going to put Darcy in an orphanage. Do they even have orphanages these days?

'Looks like it was deliberately lit,' no-balls said. 'Do you know anyone who'd want to burn your house?'

I scoffed. 'Yeah.'

'Who?' they asked together.

'Spider.'

They glanced at each other. 'Spider?'

'Martin Davis. I think that's his name.'

The guy sighed, took out a pad and pen.

The woman pulled up a chair. 'May I?'

'Of course.'

'Tell us what you can about Martin Davis.'

'How long have you got?'

Roller-derby grinned. 'As long as it takes.'

That's how I became a grass. I grassed on Spider and his grass.

Darcy was on the boob when Nev and June arrived. They knocked and I invited them in anyway.

June sat on the bed, her eyes wet.

Nev didn't know where to look.

June and I talked shit and she stroked the little man's bald head.

Seeing Nev squirm out of the corner of my eye made me feel powerful. Woman.

Nev eventually found his voice. 'Drove past your flat.'

'Gave us a hell of a fright,' June whispered. 'The lady across the road told us you were here.'

Mrs Tio's Jesus-on-the-cross was real.

'Where will you live?' June asked.

Darcy spat the nipple and burped milk on me. June offered to take him. I cleaned up and tucked myself away. He'd messed on June by then – a little bird-poo of chuck on her shoulder – but she didn't seem bothered by it.

'You could stay with us,' she said. 'Just until your place is fixed.'

'Thanks,' I said, and took the boy back. 'That's really kind. We'll see how we go.'

»—▸

The police found bodies at the back of Spider's workshop. Three bodies in plastic barrels. And half a million dollars' worth of hydro. I saw it on the news.

Emilio? Could have easily been me in a barrel.

»—▸

Darcy and I lived with June and Nev for thirty-seven days. June taught me how to cook a roast. I made Nev's sandwiches while he made goo-goo noises at the boy. I picked up a tea-drinking habit. They spoiled us. I'll never be able to repay them.

Every day – didn't matter if it was blowing a gale or pissing down rain – Darcy and I cruised past the flat on the way to the Tuvalus. We watched as the boarded-up windows became glass again and the fluoro workmen fitted a new door. The agent was there one morning, and she told me the insurance had paid for new carpets, new curtains and a coat of paint.

V

I boxed all of Mum's shit and moved into her room. My old room became the nursery. Nev helped me hang a mobile from the ceiling and put a massive giraffe sticker on the freshly painted wall. The agent said we could.

We'd been living on our own for three months when the doorbell rang. I'd just gotten the little punk to sleep and the electronic chimes woke him again. There might have been actual lightning bolts coming out of my eyes when I opened the door.

'Emilio?'

He drove his hands into his pockets. 'I'm sorry, Cassie. Sorry about the way I left you.'

'I thought you were dead.'

'So did I for a while there.'

I held the door open for him. He pecked my cheek as he entered.

I made tea while he grinned at the boy in the bouncer.

He took his cup with both hands.

'He told me he'd kill me,' Emilio said. 'I believed him.'

'He would have. You made the right choice.'

➳

My mother phoned at 3.37 am, Christmas Eve. I was up feeding the boy, so I answered it.

'Merry Christmas, ma chérie!' She sounded drunk.

'Merry Christmas.'

I could hear brass-band music in the background. And her breathing.

'Ça va?' she eventually said.

'Pardon?'

She tittered. 'Oh, I'm sorry, ma chérie, I am forgetting who I am talking with.'

Her accent had festered. She sounded faker than I remembered.

'How . . . are . . . you?'

'Fine.'

'What is the news with you?'

'Nothing much.'

Darcy stared up at me. He belched. And smiled.

My heart melted. It leaked silently out of my eyes.

'Well, I must go now,' Mum said. 'I hope you – '

Emilio staggered from the bedroom, naked. 'Who was that?'

'My mother.'

'True? What did she want?'

'Nothing.'

He rubbed his eyes and then kissed the top of my head.

'I could have given her that,' he said. 'But not at three o'clock in the morning.'

Darcy did have his father's eyes, but from the outside I looked like my mother, too.

ANOTHER THEORY OF RELATIVITY

Ryan

The experience of life is mostly a relative concept. Nothing is truly good or bad, hot or cold, wet or dry, happy or sad. These are all ideas compared and contrasted with other ideas. I know it sounds a bit fancy but stick with me – it'll be worth it.

I'm in philosophy class right now. I'm supposed to be working on my oral presentation for Mr Denver but I'm doing this instead. We had a guest speaker last lesson – a fiction writer I'd never heard of – and she got us to free write for ten minutes.

Ten minutes? Are you kidding me?

I moaned, like everybody else, but I had a crack anyway.

Something clicked. I think it was the lock on the cell door in my head. Writing free was like busting out of jail and I'm not done running yet, so hang on tight.

If some old fart drops into the train seat next to you smelling of earwax and says, 'Geez, it's cold out there,' you could say, 'Cold compared to what?' 'Cold' compared to the morning you barefooted it to the letterbox through the snow? Ice-age cold? Even the fact that the guy's an old fart is a relative term – old compared to what? 'Old' compared to you, maybe, but not old compared to the pyramids, which aren't particularly old compared to some of the rock art in the Kimberley, which in turn is a spring chicken compared to the dinosaur I just made up – *Dinosaurus old-farticus*. She just had her one hundred and fifty millionth birthday. Happy birthday to you. Hip hooray.

Speed is distance travelled over time and that shit's definitely relative. My stepdad bought me a speedo for my mountain bike last birthday, and I tested it out on Madigans Road. I mean; that hill is *steep* (compared to Bellamy Street where we live, anyway). It's a beautiful stretch of straight sealed road and I know I go as fast as I can go down that hill. Feels like a little over three hundred kilometres per hour. If my speedo's correct, it's actually seventy-six point two kph. I've slept in the back of my stepfather's car going faster than that – one hundred and ten kilometres per hour. On the dot. I've let go of my stepbrother's motorbike jacket and held my arms out (all Jesus-on-the-cross) going faster than that. Two hundred and thirty, but don't tell my stepdad. When I flew to Malawi to spend my summer doing aid work with my biological father, the in-flight stats said we were travelling at eight hundred and ninety kilometres per hour. I slept at that speed too, but not as well as the dude in the seat next to me who snored like a pig farm.

It's all relative.

No, Amanda, you are not 'fat' and your boobs are not 'too big' – you are what you are. Not that you could hear that from me – a relatively good friend, I hope – even if I had the guts to say it to your face. Do you think a perfectly happy walrus bemoans the fact that she looks ungainly in a swimsuit? Obviously, you're not a walrus but there will always be fatter and thinner walruses than you. If you eat well, move your limbs and live large, your body will be healthy and the size it's meant to be. Besides, if you really do weigh sixty kilograms on earth, then you'll only weigh nine point nine on the moon. Space travel could be the ultimate weight-loss program.

Don't get me started on boobs.

And whatever you do, don't shake your head behind Megan – the Year 8 chick in the wheelchair – and say, 'Poor girl.' I know for a fact that she hates that shit. She reckons she knows able-bodied people who suffer more than she does. Megan has a special slant on the individual and fickle nature of happiness and, for the most part, she chooses happy. For a Year 8, she has a relatively complex understanding of the way the mind works.

'Being happy is a choice you make. You can decide you're sad because you didn't get that video game you wanted for your birthday, or you can decide cake is better anyway. Nobody makes those choices for you. You do that all by yourself.'

How can you 'hate' maths? Compared to what? English? Being beaten on the bum with a car aerial? I've tried all three and I think maths has its plusses and minuses.

;-)

I wonder how much happier we would be if we got into the habit of reminding ourselves that happiness is relative?

You: Spaghetti Bolognese? Again?
Me: The fridge and pantry are loaded. Help yourself.

You: I can't fit into my favourite jeans!
Me: Man, the living has been good.

You: The internet is sooooo slowwwww.
Me: Come over here in the dirt and have a go at hitting this pointy rock with a stick. It's ace!

You: *Bang*.
Me: Ow. You made my nose bleed. I said hit the *rock!*

Still, pain is relative, too. You could have poked me in the eye or smacked my sensitive gentleman nuggets.

The fact that pain is relative isn't much consolation when you're hurting. That's probably the same with true poverty, too. Have you noticed Billy's shoes? They're all sock underneath and he won't have money for a new pair until next term – that's six weeks of winter to kick through. During the drought in Malawi, people boiled and ate the skins of animals that would have normally become shoes. Billy might know the cold better than most, but he won't have to eat his shoes. I'll make sure of that.

And finally, I arrive at the soft underparts of this idea of life being relative.

We're all relatives. (See what I did there? Poet.)

Our ancestors – I mean, absolutely every single one – strolled out of Africa a few years before my grandmother got her licence, but sometimes we forget that. Who would lock their relatives and their kids in a detention centre? What sort of monster straps explosives to himself and blows up fifty relatives on a train? A relatively misguided one, IMHO.

And if you remember back to the start of this relatively long-winded piece you'll see that I cunningly inferred that time is, in fact, relative.

Think like a rock for a minute.

That will be easier for some than others, hey Benson? Actually, scrap that; think like a stone(r) (stoner, get it? I'm on *fire*!).

Think like a piece of igneous rock, say a chunky chunk of basalt, born from the blistering womb of the planet when the seas were made entirely of lava. Man, you've seen a *lot*. You were cool before it became trendy on the surface of the earth. You were there when hydrogen and oxygen got married on *Neighbours*. You let their baby (that's water) lick your face, then wham-bam-thank-you-ma'am, water's got unicellular kids of her own and they're hanging out together playing their photosynthesisers. Next thing you know those innocent little plants have become total *animals*. They think they're so clever with their oxygen breathing and their sexual reproduction and their opposable thumbs, but we know different, don't we, rock? Rock?? Hellooooo? Seems like she's gone all shy now that the spotlight's on her, but do you see her point?

Yes, she's a pointy rock. (Ba da boom)

From a rock's perspective we're ALL related.

All the minerals, plants and animals – even Benson.

She's seen every step along the way to the infinitely complex expressions of life we now know, like Billy's shoe, Megan's wheelchair and Amanda's perfectly adequate boobs. Rock didn't have to make up some imaginary friend with superpowers to *create* all this stuff; she was there. She saw it all evolving.

That's not relative; that's *absolute*.

We are all one.

Just one planet, and we've all sprung from it. Take it back another step and you'll see that our pointy rock's ancestors were the stuff that all the stars are made of.

And we're probably a relatively complex arrangement of star-stuff, capable of quite complex thoughts like 'Chicken or beef?', '*South Park* or *Simpsons*?' and 'Why is it so?'. But if you turned off *The Simpsons* and watched the insides of your eyelids for about the same amount of time, just contemplating the interconnectedness of all living and non-living parts of the planet and our origins as star-stuff, the things that make life 'bad' or 'good' become clearer.

For example, some people have holes in their shoes and some other people have multiple pairs so there are *pockets* of relative wealth and poverty. If I offer Billy my hand-painted Heritage Volleys I get to feel kindness and Billy gets to feel dry socks, and our oneness is affirmed like a practical and cosmic high-five. There are pockets of relative hunger and pockets of obesity, pockets of ignorance and pockets of relative wisdom, sometimes in the one class-room. We've come a long way since we were rocks. Well, some of us have.

How do I know all this shit?

Well, I'm relatively gay. That might come as a shock for some – you can close your mouth now, Benson – but for others, like most of the class and like my stepdad and my stepbrother, who, it turns out, personify 'pockets of relative wisdom', my coming out was a simple statement of fact. My hair is brown. My eyes are blue. I quite like boys.

I say 'relatively gay' because human sexual preference could be the poster child for relative thinking. I can still appreciate perfectly adequate boobs (*cough*, *Amanda*), but go gaga for certain butts dancing in denim. There's a whole rainbow of experience between gay and straight and you're not nailed to the rainbow, you can dance about if you want to find out how you're wired. Even gender isn't absolute – we're not just boys and girls and you're free to sit where you like there, too.

It turns out my biological father, while a big-hearted and generous man, believes gender, sexual preference and identity are absolutes. Turns out he's also quite handy with a car aerial. A couple of thousand years ago his imaginary friend dictated a book to a few desert-dwelling relatives who were still excited about the invention of the wheelbarrow and my father treats it like ... well ... gospel. He's not alone. There are lots of people who believe their imaginary friend is the *best* and anybody who thinks differently is sick in the head and should be killed. That's a big pocket of relative ignorance, and part of me wants to just let them be. But if we're all truly related and born of the same star-stuff, then it feels like there's a growth on the back of my hand when they blah blah their bullshit. I want to get it checked out. Perhaps it will wash off, but it might be something serious.

And if we're related to the trees and rocks and air and water and animals, how can we justify destroying all our relatives' one and only home? Um, reality check – it's our one and only home, too.

Your brain is either dead or alive and if it's dead, there's no coming back from that – that's an absolute – but until you die, you're free to muck around with the all the knobs and buttons on the mixing deck of life. You can continue the tradition of filling pockets of ignorance with your relative wisdom. You can sow happy-thought-seeds wherever you go and help others remember that we're things of great beauty, rocketing through the cosmos on a thing of great beauty.

REDBEARD

Bren

I reckon it was 4 am when I woke. My phone was *dead* dead. It wouldn't even power up. The same chant I'd gone to sleep with was still there, twisting in my guts like hunger. *Fucken arseholes. They deserve each other. Fucken arseholes.* Hector's side of the tent was cold nylon and I felt relieved. *Fucken arsehole.*

A salty breeze shoved at the tea-tree overhead and covered the sound of my packing. Everything was wet. The beam of my head torch had grown so blunt by the end that I could no longer distinguish the colours of the other domes around me. Nobody stirred. I thought about using my wire saw to drop a branch through Marley's tent, hopefully wounding them both. Well, killing Hector and wounding Marley. Maybe killing them both. *Fucken arseholes*. I had the thought, but I hauled my pack on my back and walked.

My shoulders felt bruised. I tightened my waist strap and my hips and lower back felt bruised too, but it eased the weight off my shoulders. Seventeen ks to go. Maybe three hours' hike and I'd be over the mountain and back in the carpark. I'd be done before the others had even finished breakfast, providing my head torch held out. Stars winked through the canopy and the cloud cover. They were watching me, but they didn't care. Without their feeble blips I might have been underground. And then, at the bottom of a little gully, my torch *died* died and I could no longer see my hands, let alone my feet. Feeling for the track with one foot got me about three metres further on before I freaked out. Seventeen ks isn't far when you're walking the trail, but it'd be a big day if you were lost in the bush. I dropped my pack, sat on it and waited for the sun.

And waited. Maybe I'd left earlier than I thought? With my eyes peeled wide, I couldn't tell the difference between sky and ground. The stars had completely disappeared and I could smell my own armpits. This is what it's like to be blind. There was something strangely comforting about the whole scenario, like I was awake in a blank dream. The breeze didn't taste salty anymore; it was all green and brown like the forest floor. Sweet and woody. I could feel my heart beating in my fingertips. Rain dripped off the trees and found its way down my back. I shivered but I wasn't cold. I remembered that my rain jacket had a hood.

The knot of anger I'd slept with had started to soften and it felt more like proper hunger. I found a protein bar in the top pocket of my pack, skinned it, folded it and levered it into my gob. I didn't mind being Marley's 'mistake'. To be honest, those couple of hours smelling *her* sweat and feeling *her* heat were the highlight of my pathetic existence. The thing that made me clamp my jaw, the thing that made me want to punch something – or someone – was the fact that I hadn't seen it coming. I might have been her mistake, but she was my perfect. For a couple of hours, anyway. A couple of hours that could have easily become the rest of my life. I would have built a house on that ripe strawberry field of new stuff. Two hours of feeling wanted were better than none, and if the thing had to crash and burn then two hours were less painful than three. Being dumped can be a mercy.

A night-bird barked somewhere down the gully and it jolted me out of my pity party. Back in the moment, I might have been the only human left on the planet and the thought fitted like a possum-skin cloak. I'd miss Mum and Gordo, but I'd survive. Next thing, my throat's tight and tears are stinging my eyes. It's Henry I'm thinking about. Me and my little brother share one heart and I died a bit imagining he might be alone. I had to paint over that thought with a more likely scenario: he's star-fished and asleep in his bed, his quilt and his pyjamas are twisted around him and his belly is exposed. His stomach's rising and falling with the bright rhythm of his little-kid breathing. He's okay.

There were bound to be some awkward conversations between here and home. I'd be two and a half hours on the bus with Hector and Marley. We could ignore each other, but Marley isn't good with silence. She'd hiked five days with a spare battery for her phone so she could sleep with her singer-songwriter playlist. I had no words for her. I didn't know what I'd say to Hector. Maybe a brief rant in full-contact body language?

Just when I thought the darkness might go on forever, the clouds and the trees began to peel apart. As the branches became distinct silhouettes, I could see the rift in the canopy made by the track. I still couldn't see my feet, but I could imagine where they needed to go, so I packed up and walked the path mirrored in the sky. It was slow going, but it was *going*. The movement and the uneven trail gave my head something to do. My calves and hamstrings burned – the only obvious sign that I was picking my way up Mount Fitzgerald. Wim, our outdoor education teacher, had said that this last day, day six of six, was the hardest day. It was only seventeen ks but more than half of them were uphill. Sometimes being blind eases the burden of what lies ahead.

The world gradually appeared out of the darkness. The contrast shifted and birds began whispering in the undergrowth. There was something pleasing about being the first human awake in that neck of the woods. Awake before the sun and before the morning birds found their full voice. Before they were awake enough to fly. The suckers back at camp would still be snoring and the ks were already racking up behind me. I had a jump on them and a jump on the day. We'd be out of sync. I'd be more awake than them for hours. While the light seemed grey and muted, colour began to creep into the bushes and the path. I could see my feet and I watched them doing their thing – one after the other – for quite some time. It was hard to tell if the drops rapping on the nylon of my pack had been blown out of the trees or had come straight from the clouds. That was until the canopy briefly opened up and I was still getting wet. I yanked the strings on my hood and watched my feet some more.

The first track marker I could read said MF3. MF2 arrived soon after that. I thought MF1 had been plucked out of the ground and thrown into the bushes, but it eventually turned up. I could feel my pulse in my mouth. I sucked my drinking bladder dry and then emptied my actual bladder on the marker. I didn't take my pack off. I walked.

While that last kilometre to the top of Mt Fitzgerald might have been the longest k of my life, there was still no sign of the actual sun. Not until I cleared the bushes and the track flattened into a clearing the size of a basketball court, a viewing platform perched at the far end. I shucked off my pack and leaned on the stainless-steel rail. That's when the sun peeked through. A gap in the hurtling clouds sprayed the motley view with a fan of orange light and illuminated a bloke sitting beside the platform. I hadn't noticed him when I arrived. He hadn't said anything. He leaned against his pack and squinted at the light like he wasn't game to move, wasn't game to disturb the moment. For a full minute the sunlight shifted and danced around us, turning the rain on the leaves into jewels. A parrot the colour of noon sky and oxygenated blood landed on the rail beside me. It was close enough to pat but I didn't. We watched each other for ten seconds or so, then the bird blew its umpire's whistle and was gone. I felt the air from its wings on the back of my hand. I glanced at the bloke, but he was unmoved. He stared at the clouds that swallowed the sun, the wind buffeting his beard. He looked tired.

No.

The thought punched through the clouds of exhaustion in my own head like a firecracker dawn.

He didn't look tired.

I cleared my throat louder than I needed to. 'Morning.'

Rain had pooled in the dirty cup of his upturned right hand.

I crouched, patted his shoulder. 'Okay, mate?'

He was maybe thirty-five, tops. Tufts of bright red hair protruded from the edges of a brown knitted beanie. The eyes I thought were squinting were rolled into his head and the skin exposed above his beard reminded me of egg-shells. Not free-range but rare museum eggs the colour of high summer cloud. And his beard: what a beard. A wild man's beard. Just the orange side of old blood, it hung to his breastbone. Several small twigs and a yellow leaf were tangled in there, as though a night creature had begun to make a nest. Probably just the wind. His legs were crossed loosely like he'd sat on the bare earth before and knew how to get comfortable. His leather boots had done some ks.

He was okay, yes, but dead.

Dead dead.

It was nothing like the movies. I didn't recoil, I didn't run, and I certainly didn't scream. Death was nothing like I'd imagined, and I squatted there staring until it began to rain. Proper rain. The sort of downpour that would make you thankful for roofs and windows and doors, if you had any. The water splashed off the bloke's cheeks and ran shining down the side of his neck. He seemed like the sort of bloke who enjoyed the rain, but as the squall got serious, I wished I had an umbrella to share. I did, sort of. I unrolled my wet tent and used it like a tarp for both of us. I knocked the bloke's beanie over his eyes and straightened it without thinking, like the dead man was my little brother.

He didn't smell dead. He smelled like clean sweat and wet wool and I knew he'd be missed. He was maybe someone's brother, certainly someone's son and the freckles on the back of his hand looked like paint flecks, as if he'd taken a break from his latest creation to climb Mount Fitzgerald. And die. He didn't look like he'd planned to check out. If it was a suicide, he'd gone the extra mile to hide the evidence. There was no blood. There were no empty pill bottles or tell-tale rope. In fact, it looked like he'd been living a good life.

It stopped raining briefly, long enough for me to properly set my tent up beside the viewing platform. I thought about dragging the man into the shelter, but I didn't know where to start on a project like that. The heavens opened again and in an uncommon fit of genius, I unzipped the door, picked up the whole tent and put it over the man. It covered him completely. The rain pecked and then shhhhed on the nylon. It cried onto the wet earth, collected in tiny rivulets and snaked off down the slope. The wetter I got, the drier he seemed.

'You must have left early.'

I flailed and my reaction made Ang Butler laugh. I hadn't heard him coming over the sound of rain on my hood.

'What's with the tent? You camp here last night?'

'No. It's ... I was trying to get it dry.'

He laughed again. 'How's that working out for you?'

I shrugged. 'Where's everybody else?'

'Coming,' he said. He rested his elbows on the handrail. 'Wim's full of shit. He reckoned the view was spectacular. Said you can see the ocean. All I can see is fucken clouds.'

The breeze shifted and the rain was in our faces.

'Fuck this,' Ang spat, and left.

It was maybe half an hour before anybody else arrived. The rain had stopped, and I'd pulled my hood off. I heard them coming. Two guys, four girls, shouting and laughing. They were the Nerrima West football-netball crew in their leggings and compression shorts. They shed their packs and converged on the viewing platform like it was half-time and I was invisible.

They talked among themselves and I understood what they were saying but it sounded like flies buzzing to my ears. They were complete as a group. They spat out words to avoid the silence. I knew they could see me, but I also knew they wouldn't choose to look. My tent rattled in the breeze.

He wasn't really a secret, the dead man. I'd tell them if they asked. The tent felt like closing the toilet door for Henry when his big boy wee escalates into a big boy poo. Like Henry, the dead man didn't care if the door was open. The tent made life simpler for those left alive.

They picked up their gear like they were a single organism.

As they left, Marley and Hector arrived. She dropped his hand and thumbed her pack straps. Hector looked everywhere but at me. I saw all that from the corner of my eye and felt nothing. Nothing. Redbeard in the tent had changed the game.

They rested their packs against the stainless-steel posts of the viewing platform. I was the elephant in that room. I greeted them both without saying a thing. Hector dug through his pack. Marley stood beside me, hands on the rail, elbows locked. I could hear her breathing.

'I'm sorry,' she said. It wasn't much more than a whisper.

'It's fine.'

'I never meant …'

'Honestly, it's fine. Don't worry about it.'

Hector propped on the other side of me, peeling an orange. 'And I'm sorry, too. We didn't plan it.'

I shrugged. 'You've got to do what feels right.'

They both stared. I squinted against the view like the man in the tent. The sun sliced through the canopy of grey cloud for a few seconds. A highlighter of hope.

'Drying your tent?' Hector asked.

'Shed a few kilos of rainwater.'

'Good idea,' Marley said. 'I couldn't be bothered. We'll be home soon enough.'

Hector offered me a segment of his orange. I took it. It tasted like that ray of sunshine.

Parko – the other outdoor ed teacher – appeared out of the bushes closely followed by her shadow, May Lennox. May did a couple of star jumps when she made it to the viewing platform. We exchanged muted high-fives.

'All downhill from here, guys,' Parko said.

'Whose tent?' May asked.

I held up my hand.

'Don't really need to dry it out,' Parko said. 'You'll be in your own bed tonight.'

I nodded. 'Where's Wim?'

'Mr van der Velden's with Alice,' May said.

'Her feet were hurting,' Parko added. 'They're not far behind. Everything okay?'

'Yeah,' I said, a little too brightly. I did the maths. Wim and Alice were the last.

Hector finished his orange and punched into his pack. Marley followed suit. They didn't say goodbye, but it didn't really matter. Nothing really mattered. For a minute it looked like Parko and May were going to follow them out, but they stopped beside my tent, set up their stove and cooked some noodles. They chatted and joked like they'd been hanging out for six years, not six days. Parko wiped her fork on her shorts and offered me a dig at their noodle mess. I ate. Well, I burned my mouth, spat noodles into my hand and juggled them until they were cool enough to swallow.

'Can we cook some more?' May asked.

Parko's shoulders dropped. 'Seriously?'

'Not for me,' May explained. 'I want to feed the monkey again. That was hilarious.'

I bared my teeth, pelted her with imaginary poo.

⤞

They'd been gone ten minutes when the long streak of Wim and pink-haired Alice arrived. Alice had one of Wim's hiking poles. She was limping, but not like she had been the day before. Her eyes looked bright, hopeful even. Not a sign of a tear. She dropped her pack at the edge of the clearing and sat on it.

For one reason or another, my chest grew tight. The dead man hadn't been a secret, but the thought of revealing him to Wim stole my breath like the mountain had.

His brow furrowed as he drew close. 'Everything okay?'

My throat locked. I swiped at my eyes, shook my head.

He clamped a hand on my shoulder and regarded me with his blue-pen eyes.

'Do you have the sat-phone?' I asked.

'Ja, you know I do. What's the problem?'

'I found a dead man.'

⤞

We were on the opposite side of the clearing, but Alice looked away as they loaded Redbeard into the air ambulance. She gripped my fingers. Her hair flapped about in the downwash from the helicopter. And when they were done and gone, with no chance of a lift to the carpark, we shouldered our bags and walked.

THE THING

Amy

I believe in like at first sight.

The photo Adam showed me while we were waiting for Kazu at the airport looked as though it was taken in juvie. Who doesn't like a bad boy? And then, as he stepped through the arrival gates and our eyes met for the first time, I could tell he wasn't a true bad boy. He wasn't a Japanese gangster – yakuza – he was more like a new puppy you couldn't trust with your furniture. He was mischief. I like mischief.

In the car on the way home, Adam chose the front seat. It was his turn, so I didn't fight him, but it was a poor choice for a host. It meant I had two-and-a-half hours in the back with Kazu and, like that new puppy, he imprinted on me instead of my brother. That, combined with the fact that I've always been better at Japanese than

Adam, meant his role as the exchange host was more of a ceremonial position. Adam looked better on paper. He hadn't spent a single night in hospital. He hadn't missed a day of school.

Ray reckoned it wasn't 'like', it was 'love'; she may have been right, but it wasn't 'love' like she meant it. I'm not wired like that. There aren't enough gradations in English to define our relationship in a single word. It was kind of brother–sister 'love', but it got weird.

Around our fourteenth breakfast together, Mum was digging in Kazu's bag for his lunchbox. She recoils and squeaks like she's seen a spider, right?

'What?' Adam asks, and Mum just shakes her head.

She's looking at her empty hand and she's glaring at Kazu.

Adam tilts open the top of Kazu's pack with a single finger and peers inside, then his head retracts and he's backing away too. 'Nasty,' he says.

Kazu's brow is scrunched. He slides his bag closer, pinches both sides of the zip and looks in. He's still puzzled, but now his eyes seem to be sparkling. Mischief. He dives in and pulls out a dirty pink dildo. He's holding it with a tad more confidence than you'd expect from a sixteen-year-old exchange student – in fact he's gripping it like a microphone.

I do an involuntary Mum-squeak and slide off my chair. Next thing I know he's waving it in my face. I'm off down the hallway and he's chasing me into the lounge. He's laughing.

Mum and Adam are yelling for him to stop and when it finally sinks in his face changes colour and he skulks back to the kitchen.

He tells me he's sorry. He tells Mum and Adam, too, but nobody knows what to say so nobody says anything. The thing disappears and ten minutes later we're hustling out the door like nothing's happened.

I remember to tell Ray the story at lunchtime and she shakes her head. 'Sick.'

I agree, but Kazu isn't the sick one. He seemed genuinely surprised to find it in his bag. Surprised, but not freaked out by it like the rest of us. I realised he was chasing me the way I'd chased him with the open can of dog food the week before. The manky silicone penis was next-level gross.

Adam and I have been in the same year since he repeated Year 1. It's a fact I like to remind him of regularly. At home. In private. They put us in the same class in Year 3 and it didn't end well. I lost some hair. Adam lost a tooth that wasn't quite ready to fall out on its own. It's a fact he likes to remind me of regularly. We get to

Year 10 and we end up in Design Tech together. Sharp tools, heavy hammers: there are lots of weapons in the woodwork and metalwork rooms. It's three classes a week and we act like we don't know each other. That's how we handle lunchtimes and sports days, too.

Kazu complicates that. He stands with Ray and me and he does nothing. He plays games on his phone while Mr Charalambous isn't watching; that is, until Mr Charalambous catches him and confiscates his phone. Now he does *absolutely* nothing. Says nothing. His face – his whole body, really – is sagging. Charalambous tries to get him started on a project, and for a few minutes he's nodding and collecting wood and tools, but it doesn't last. I don't need an interpreter to read his body language. I consult my English–Japanese dictionary and pencil a word in katakana on a timber offcut. I hand it to Kazu.

'What does it say?' Ray asks.

'I don't know,' Kazu says, but at least he's smiling.

'What's it supposed to say?' Ray asks.

I shrug. 'Doesn't matter.'

Her eyes are wide, and she elbows me.

Kazu spends the rest of the lesson drawing over and over the word on the wood. Charalambous shouts for us to pack up and Kazu puts the offcut in his bag. He's staring at me, his face slack. He nods once and says the word I'd written.

'Hōmushikku.'

Homesick.

↠

It's discouraged by the people who manage the exchange program, but that night we set Kazu up to Skype with his family. I can't keep up with the conversation but there's laughter and tears and by the end Kazu seems taller. Straighter. Stronger. He props in the bathroom doorway while I'm brushing my teeth. He has the timber offcut.

'Thank you,' he says.

I lift a shoulder and spit in the sink as discreetly as I can.

'Smell,' he says, offering up the small block of wood.

It's pine. It's sweet. It's clean.

'Smells like my father,' he says.

We talk for hours after that. Really talk. His father is an artist. He works in wood. He builds furniture. I tell him I was in hospital before he came. I stumble when he asks me why. I get my English–Japanese dictionary.

Utsubyō.

Depression.

↠

Kazu *arrived* after that. He said yes to everything and everybody. Seemed like every time I saw him, he was hanging with another crew. Playing footy with the Year 11s or downball with the 7s, he didn't care and, to be fair, neither did they. He was hungry. Hungry for every new experience. Hungry for company. Hungry for food. Even Vegemite. If I'm honest, I missed him when he went off with the boys on the weekends. If I'm honest, I felt like spraying the Year 9 scrags with the fire extinguisher when they made him laugh so hard he changed colour. If I'm honest, I couldn't wait for design tech.

Kazu eventually settled on a project. He and Mr Charalambous grew tight. The project was a big secret. Charalambous brought him some Japanese dozuki saws from his home workshop. Kazu spent that entire double lesson bowing at the teacher any time he came close. Kazu took to measuring, cutting and sanding long after the bell told us to go home. He walked home by himself a few times when I got sick of waiting.

He beat me home once. I found him in the bathroom, scrubbing furiously at something in the sink.

The dildo.

He sucked breath and tried to close the door. 'Sorry, Amy, sorry. Don't look.'

'What are you doing?'

'Cleaning.'

'I can see that. Why are you cleaning that … thing?'

'For a gift.'

'Gift?'

His eyes sparkled. He nodded.

'Do you want a hand?'

'But . . . you don't like this. You are scared?'

I took the wet toy from him. It was heavier than I expected. A weapon.

I tapped it on his forehead. 'Not scared. Pretending. I'm not as innocent as I seem.'

'So,' he said. 'This I believe.'

I smacked him in the head again – properly this time – and shoved him through to the laundry.

Kazu told me his plan and we took it in turns to bleach and scrub the phallus.

It was a good plan. A smart plan. Mischief.

'Where did it even come from? How did it end up in your bag?'

'Joke,' Kazu said. 'Caleb and Ben So made a joke. Caleb is not so smart. Ben is not so smart.'

That made sense. Caleb and Ben had broken into Ray's locker when we were in Year 8 and peeled and stuck a full pack of her panty liners on the outside of her locker door.

'Bad joke. Good for me.'

He dried the thing with Adam's towel, inspecting it like a craftsman.

'Ho!' he said, laughing.

He showed me the base where a single word had been moulded into the silicone.

Nippon.

'Not everything is made in China!' he said.

➳

I helped Kazu with his speech, with the English and what he wanted to say. I listened while he practised.

He threw down his notes.

'I wish I could make speech in Japanese. You could translate.'

'You're doing fine, Kazu.'

'But it is for the whole school.'

'Sometimes your English is better than mine. Get over yourself.'

➳

Mrs Johnson, the exchange coordinator, made her introduction.

'The exchange program we have at Nerrima High is a source of great pride for us. Each year we host one student from our sister school Kawasaki High near Tokyo in Japan. It's a bit of a lottery. We never know what our visiting students are going to be like. I think you'll all agree with me that this year we won the lottery. Ladies and gentlemen, I give you Kazunobu Hanaki.'

There was a brief ripple of applause. Kazu arranged his notes on the stand, bowed and hit his head on the microphone.

There was laughter. My heart pounded.

'Thank you, Mrs Johnson, and thank you Dr Cunningham, staff and students. I have learned many things during my time in Australia. I have learned how to ride a kangaroo, wrestle a crocodile and make love to a sheep.'

Dr Cunningham, the principal, seated next to Kazu on stage, laughed and covered his mouth. The rest of the audience weren't so polite.

'I have discovered local delicacies like a pot and parma at the Royal, a pie and sauce at the footy and a slab of VB with the boys. I have learned how to drop the kids off at the pool, do doughies in the paddock bomb and I know which way to run when someone yells, "COPS!"'

The laughter wasn't so small anymore.

'But I'm kidding. Aren't I?'

'I hope so,' Dr Cunningham said.

'Near to my home in Kawasaki there is a very famous temple called Kanayama Shrine. It is famous for a festival called Kanamara Matsuri which means festival of the steel phallus. Steel penis.'

Mrs Johnson let out a squeak. I hoped it was laughter.

'During the festival people wear penis costumes, carry giant penises and eat penis-shape food. They raise money for HIV research and have many laughs.'

'Perhaps we can arrange a school excursion?' Mrs Johnson shouted.

'It is this shrine, this festival, this part of my culture that has inspired my omiyage. My souvenir gift to you, Dr Cunningham.'

'I'm not sure I like where this is going, Kazu,' Dr Cunningham said.

'Please,' Kazu said, and invited him up to share the stand. He handed him his wrapped gift.

'With the help of Mr Charalambous, I have made a gift for the school.'

'I see.'

'Open. It's not a snake.'

He tore the paper. He laughed. He held the gift aloft.

A beautifully handcrafted timber box with a glass front containing a shiny pink silicone penis.

'My very good friends Caleb and Ben So . . . where are they? Down here! Caleb and Ben provided the penis from their personal collection. Made in Japan. It was a very big sacrifice. Thank you, Caleb. Thank you, Ben.'

Kazu made prayer hands. The audience clapped and roared. All except Caleb and Ben.

Dr Cunningham shook Kazu's hand and bent the microphone up to his mouth. His eyes were shiny.

'Thank you, Kazu. I'm not sure where we'll be able to display your gift, but we'll find a place. It is a beautiful thing. I mean *the case*. The case is beautifully crafted. You did this yourself?'

Kazu bowed.

The applause from the crowd had begun with hands and now moved down their bodies to include their feet stomping on the auditorium floor. I felt it in my knees and in my heart. I'm sure Kazu did, too.

It was a beautiful thing.

KARMA

Ang

Mum's boyfriend, Brent, is the exact opposite of my father. When they split up, Mum rebounded like one of those massive rubber bouncy balls from the vending machine at Central. Dad's a welfare worker with the Jensen Foundation – his day job is saving lost souls. Brent works with Mum in juvie. Dad plays classical violin. Brent's idea of 'music' is his Harley-Davidson Fat Boy, idling. Seriously, they're nemesis cartoon characters. Yeah, and it turns out Dad likes younger men. Brent likes older women. Brent wins the handshake every time they meet. Dad doesn't seem to care.

They r both fuckwits, Taylor texted.

It made me LOL and Mum grinned from the passenger seat.

'What?'

'Nothing,' I said, and punched my sister in the thigh.

Common enemies had made us friends for the first time in years.

We were in the back seat of Brent's Yank Tank – a crew-cab Ram utility that played the same song as the Fat Boy – and he'd given us protective booties to wear over our thongs while we were in the car. That's where his world and Mum's overlapped – I grew up thinking boys were supposed to sit down to pee. Thanks, Mum.

We were heading for Brent's 'block' to 'go feral'. I wanted to like Brent, but he made it difficult. Taylor (fourteen years old) and me (fifteen) had negotiated the shit out of being allowed to stay home, but Mum works in youth detention and knows every trick in the book. Plus, she has cuffs. And capsicum spray. It was the summer holidays and all our friends were at the beach. I ran into Dale's grandma at Central and she told me that he was with his folks in Bali. No wonder he didn't text back. Chloe Veno said Taylor could stay with her. Apparently, my sister wasn't that desperate.

Brent's block fronted the Princeton River behind Maybeline, and it smelled so much better than the multi-air-freshener ute. There were march flies and bull ants, but the water was so clear I could see fish. The campsite was flat and shaded.

'What's with all the empty beer cans?' Taylor asked.

'Swim first, ask questions later,' Brent said. He stripped to his board shorts. His flabby body was a patchwork of half-done tribal tattoos, like a drunk had attacked him with a permanent marker. He ran and dived from a rock on the river's edge – a move straight out of the *How to Break Your Neck* handbook – but he came back up again.

He stood waist deep and shook his shaggy head. 'Come on, you softcocks, it's awesome.'

Mum and Taylor used each other for balance as they stepped into the rocky shallows dressed in shorts and T-shirts.

I should have gone in. I *would* have gone in, but I noticed Brent playing with the tie on the front of his board shorts. He bobbed for a bit, just his head poking out, then swung his shorts in the air.

'Woohoo!'

Mum laughed, but there was no humour in it.

'Gross,' Taylor mumbled.

The water didn't conceal much. He didn't appear to have any pubic hair.

'Spare the kids, Brent,' Mum said. 'Put it away.'

'In a minute,' Brent said. 'Feel free to look elsewhere, kids.'

He squatted neck-deep again and his face changed. His eyes narrowed; his lips puckered. He looked like he was . . .

'What are you doing?' Taylor asked, monotone. 'Are you . . .?'

Then his face changed again, to a grin of relief. He sighed.

'Oh my god,' Taylor said. 'You didn't.'

'What?' Brent said, and jogged upstream a little. He glanced over his shoulder and jogged some more. 'It's chasing me,' he howled.

Then I saw it – a foot of turd bobbing in his wake.

Taylor squealed. It was a sound I hadn't heard for years but it summed up exactly how I felt.

'What?' Brent said. 'All ends up in the ocean eventually.'

Taylor scrabbled for shore, gagging and moaning. Mum just stood there, hands on her hips. I could see she was still smiling, but if she was a dog, I wouldn't be patting her. That smile was *savage*. I left her and Brent and Brent's turd and his ghostly junk and went back to the car with Taylor. Our phones had no signal, so we had to talk out loud.

'What does she see in him?' she asked.

'He's not Dad.'

'Is he even human?'

'Primitive. Possibly *Homo erectus*.'

'Ha! Dad would be happy. Loves an erect homo.'

We fell into an awkward silence.

'Those thoughts are better left to burn out in your head,' I said.

'Oh, sorry,' she said. 'Sorry, little princess.'

'Don't get me wrong,' I said. 'It was clever ... and probably accurate.'

'Thank you.'

'But he's our dad. It's sad. I think he's being brave.'

'I deleted his music,' she sighed.

'Harsh.'

She slapped a march fly that had been feasting on her ankle and ground it into the dirt with the toe of her thong. 'I'm allowed to be pissed off.'

'Yup,' I said. 'Me too. I don't think he did it to piss us off.'

»—▸

Mum and Brent came back from the river half an hour later, holding hands.

I felt sick.

'Thought you guys would have the tents up by now,' Brent said. 'Chop chop.'

'Wouldn't know where to start,' Taylor said.

Mum knew where to start – as Brent got busy unpacking, she sanitised her hands and forearms and changed under her towel into dry clothes.

There were *guns* in the back of the ute. Two guns – a rifle and a shotgun. And chainsaw*s*. Plural. Maybe the water hadn't distorted the size of Brent's junk and he really was compensating?

He cocked the rifle and inspected the breech like they do in the movies, brought it to his shoulder and fired a shot. At a *tree*. Admittedly, the tree looked pretty dead, but seriously? Mum and Taylor hadn't seen it coming and they yelped at the noise. Birds scattered, and above us in another tree, claws raked on bark. Brent and I saw it at the same time – a possum, rudely awakened by the gunshot and now heading for cover.

Brent took aim.

'Don't!' I howled, but he shot it anyway.

It bounced off branches as it fell and hit the ground with a sickening thump.

'What the fuck?' I said.

Brent grinned. 'Not bad, hey? They're pests in New Zealand.'

'We're not in New Zealand.'

Mum's mouth hung open as Brent lifted the possum by its tail.

'Can we leave?' Taylor asked. 'Now.' She sounded like she was five.

'What?' Brent said, chuckling. 'It's a possum! We can cook him up and eat him if you like.'

He dropped it at my feet. 'Got a knife? I've got a knife.'

And in that moment, I saw straight through him. He was a semi-grown-up version of Caleb Dennis or Ben

So – guys from school who only felt alive when they were pissing people off.

'I'll watch,' I said.

I could hear Taylor pleading with Mum. Mum was rapidly running out of legit reasons to stay.

Brent butchered the butchering. The poor possum became a bloody mess.

'We'll collect a bit of firewood before it gets dark,' Brent said, wiping his hands on an old blue towel. He grabbed one of the chainsaws and it started third try.

The bawling engine sent Taylor scurrying up the track towards the road.

Brent, in his thongs and damp board shorts, squared up at the base of the tree he'd shot.

'You don't need to cut a tree down!' I shouted. 'There's plenty of wood lying around.'

He waved me off.

I grabbed my bag from the back seat, and Taylor's too.

The tree he'd shot wasn't as big as some of the others on the block, but my hands wouldn't have touched around it if I'd given it a hug.

I *wanted* to hug it.

Sawdust flew as he expertly carved a wedge of wood from one side. He inspected the trunk some more, peered into the bush where the tree would fall and began his final cut.

Taylor covered her ears.

I held my breath.

The tree cracked.

The saw stalled, stuck in the cut.

Brent swore.

The tree cracked again.

Brent swore some more and ran. Hard. As hard and fast as his fat little legs could carry him. He lost a thong, but he didn't stop.

The tree groaned and finally fell – right on top of his car.

Metal crunched and glass shattered. Camping gear was flung high into the air and rained down around him.

As the last of it fluttered earthwards, Brent grabbed his hair. 'Fuuuuck!'

The three of us – Mum, Taylor and me – applauded.

Mum only stopped cheering to pick her phone from her pocket and take a photo.

'Let's get out of here,' she said.

→

I suppose we walked for an hour before we found signal. I got Mum to send us the pic before she phoned Aunty Kim. We ate at a truck stop outside Maybeline and laughed so hard at the image of the busted ute that we cried. The tears started with the laughter, but Taylor got too close to the edge and started crying for real. She dragged Mum and me over.

By the time Kim arrived, we'd cried ourselves dry.

Mum showed her sister the picture and the laughter was back.

For good.

BONE MOON

Jack

'Where's Wim?' I asked.

'Mr van der Velden has retired for the evening,' Parko said. She sounded more like the hired help in a British period drama than my outdoor education teacher.

'Retired?'

'Indeed.'

We laughed and she took a swig from her silver plastic pouch.

I blinded her with my head torch. Again.

'May I have some?' I asked. I could smell it on her breath. 'My parents are French,' I lied. 'We have wine at every meal.'

Parko furtively scanned the camp. It was only us. Everybody else had retreated to their tents and dined on the last of their chips and dried noodles. She thought about it, and then slipped her contraband back into her internal jacket pocket.

'Come on,' I moaned.

'I am not your parent,' Parko enunciated. 'This is not gay Pareee.'

The wind had dropped. It hadn't rained for half an hour. Our communal cooking tarp crinkled overhead. Limecutters Bay coughed and roared from the other side of the dunes. I stirred my pot.

'That smells divine, Jack.'

'Postmodern fusion,' I said. I'd been thinking about that phrase since our lunch stop.

'Listen to you! Day-five gourmet. Postmodern fusion?'

'Shiitake risotto.'

'Japanese mushrooms with Italian rice. Bravo.'

I didn't have to explain myself to Parko.

'Wish I had a few tablespoons of wine to deglaze it.'

'Hoh! You watch too much food porn,' Parko said. She took her pouch from her pocket and splashed some into the pot. It hissed and the steam went straight to my salivary glands.

'Would you like some?'

Parko scoffed. 'No, I couldn't. You carted your shiitake all this way, you deserve it.'

'Dried mushrooms. They weigh nothing. Please. There's more than I can eat.'

'What about Mitchell?'

'Mitch ate noodles and canned tuna while *I* put up the tent. He's probably asleep.'

Parko dusted a green plastic bowl with her fingers and arranged it on the damp sand next to mine.

'If it's not too much trouble.'

'Not at all, mademoiselle.'

'You're too kind.'

Parko spat her first forkful back into her bowl. Her cheeks flushed and she fanned her mouth.

'Why did you make it so hot?'

'Terribly sorry,' I said. 'One of the side effects of cooking.'

She necked her silver pouch then handed it to me. I sipped and held it in my mouth while she replaced the lid. I nodded my approval and swallowed. It tasted like naughty white wine.

We blew on our food and ate in relative silence.

Parko eventually moaned and shook her head. She dropped her empty bowl and smacked her lips.

'You carried cracked black pepper for forty-three kilometres?'

'Such a burden.'

'It's not the weight I'm impressed by, it's the *forethought*. The planning. The vision. Normally day-five meals consist of broken biscuits and stale bread. A touch of Parmesan, a sprinkle of parsley and I would have paid good money for that at a restaurant.'

'Stop it, I'm blushing.'

'Blush away. I can't see a thing with your head torch in my face.'

'Sorry.'

Parko provided the scourer and went to town cleaning the bottom of the pot.

'Ah, so that's what clean looks like?'

'Take notes, Jack. Share them around.'

And just like that, she was my teacher again.

Straight-backed, I nested the pot with the others and zipped the stove in its bag.

'Thank you for the po-mo risotto,' Parko said. 'That will go down in the Nerrima High camping culinary Hall of Fame.'

'Wow, honoured. There's a Hall of Fame?'

'More like a plaque.'

'Still . . .'

'Well, there *should* be a plaque. That was amazing.'

'Pleasure.'

'I shall bid you good night,' she said, all chambermaid again. 'Must do my tent round before I retire. Break up any wrestling matches.'

Her wrestling matches wore air quotes.

'Indeed,' I said. I'd barely heard a sound from the collection of coloured domes since we'd eaten. No head torches flashing, no zips howling, nothing.

'Goodnight.'

I woke to the nylon rustle of Mitch packing his sleeping bag, as I had for the last five mornings. I could just make out his shape. There were no birds singing.

'It's the middle of the night,' I grumbled.

'Ten to five,' he said. 'Time to go home.'

I clicked my light on.

Mitch squinted and grinned, all teeth and crazy hair. 'Did you sleep with your head torch on your head?'

'Maybe.'

I thought about rolling over but the mention of home set something fizzing in my guts. I hatched out of my cocoon and stuffed it into its bag for the last time. We rolled our sleeping mats and packed the damp tent like professionals, the white noise and thunder of the ocean masking the sounds of our industry. We ate the last of the Weetbix with powdered milk, washed our bowls and spoons and still nobody stirred.

Mitch shouldered his pack. 'Let's go.'

'Wim said we have to walk together.'

'Who cares what Wim says?'

I put up my hand.

'Hopeless,' he said, and dropped his pack. 'Let's go down the beach then.'

'We should let somebody know.'

He dragged me by the sleeve. 'They'll work it out.'

I didn't really need my head torch – a bone-coloured three-quarter moon made the sandy trail glow – but there was something comforting about the detail my light revealed around us. I turned it off when we got to the bay – the smooth wet stones glossed like eyes under the moonlight. We picked our way south over the rocks into the wind-shadow of the headland. It felt warmer closer to the weathered sandstone, and the paving of pebbles and boulders gave way to patches of tide-groomed sand.

I could see bare footprints. Fresh ones. If Mitch noticed them, he didn't say anything, but they puzzled me. We were in the middle of the Magellan. We hadn't seen anybody else since the first day. We'd arrived at sunset the evening before, in the rain. It seemed like the whole crew had put up their tents and just climbed in. I thought Parko and I had been the only stayers. Mitch and I were the only early birds. A hundred metres or so from the point, the sandstone wall beside us became pitted and eroded. Large chunks of the escarpment, carved by wind and water, had slumped towards the ocean and been blunted by the waves.

'Cool,' Mitch breathed. He stopped on the fallen sandstone to admire a hole in the headland. A smooth-mouthed sea-cave. The opening was only a metre tall, but three, maybe four metres wide.

'You go first,' Mitch said, and slapped my back.

'Me?'

He pointed to my head torch. 'I'll be right behind you.'

I switched the light on and dropped to my knees in front of that toothless maw. The footprints in the sand entered the cave but didn't come out again.

'Cooee?'

The waves hushed behind us. The light didn't reach the back of the cave, but I could see that it got taller inside. I ducked under the lip and crawled until I could crouch.

'Hello?'

'What do you see?' Mitch bellowed.

I didn't answer right away – I'd been distracted by the panicked rustling of nylon, the sound of a body moving in the shadows. A step further in, I could stand. One more step and I discovered the source of the animal noises – Aaden Dualeh. He squinted, sleepy-eyed at the light.

'Who is that?' he asked.

'It's me,' I whispered. 'Jack.'

He sighed and pulled the unzipped sleeping bag over his head. The action exposed his dark-skinned feet.

And another set of bare toes.

'What time is it?' Aaden asked.

'Early. Maybe six or something.'

'What is it?' Mitch yelled from outside.

Two empty water bottles lay toppled in the sand near Aaden's covered head. A scattering of mint wrappers and deflated balloons surrounded their makeshift bed. They'd had quite a last-night party. That was when I realised the mint wrappers weren't mint wrappers and the balloons weren't balloons at all. It had been a completely different sort of last-night party. I suddenly felt like I was in Aaden's bedroom. I'd been in Aaden's *actual* bedroom before – we were friends in primary school. Back then, his walls were lined with posters of soccer players and his floor was lined with discarded soccer gear.

'What is it?' Mitch shouted again.

Aaden's head burst from beneath the covers, his eyes wide.

'Who is that?' he whispered.

'Mitchell.'

'Mother of Mary,' Aaden hissed. He scrambled to dress under the sleeping bag and in doing so revealed the owner of the feet that shared his bed.

Tariq Kattan?

Naked?

I looked away and disturbed a small group of birds that had been roosting on the wall of the cavern. They circled around my head, peeping in fear, then flew for the opening. I followed them out into the milky daylight.

Mitchell swore and slapped at his head. 'Bats!'

'Birds. They've gone. You can relax. Come on. Let's head back.'

I grabbed the sleeve of his hoodie and dragged him over the fallen sandstone.

➳

We set off as a group just after eight. The tight track meant walking single file. The banter present at the start of the hike had dried up. Mikayla Dalton had stopped complaining about her feet, but she hadn't stopped walking.

Discovering Aaden and Tariq together tasted like naughty white wine. I'd accidentally become part of their secret and so many things snapped into focus. That's why Aaden had been allowed to share a tent with Mikayla: Mikayla knew. Maybe Wim knew too? Parko knew. Maybe Parko even knew that Aaden and Tariq were into each other? I wondered if Aaden's mum and dad knew. His coach? His teammates? Why should they? What business was it of theirs? Surely whatever –

'Jack!' Parko said. 'Sorry, didn't mean to startle you.'

'No, it's fine. I just . . .'

'You were a million miles away. How are you holding up?'

'Good, yeah. Good.'

She looked at her watch. 'Only about four ks to go. Think you'll make it?'

'Easy,' I said, clenched my fists and marched on.

'Good man,' Parko said. She barged beside me and strode after Mitch. He wasn't far in front.

You know someone's secret and you have power over them. I wondered what would happen if I told Dr Cunningham – the principal – that Parko had supplied me with wine on the outdoor education camp. I wondered what would happen if I told Mrs Dualeh about the way her son liked to party. Mrs Dualeh scared me when I was little. She had rules about elbows on tables and rules about saying grace. I was carrying an egg for Aaden – something thin-shelled and filled with the rancid judgement of others. How is that even a *thing* in this day and age? There was no doubting it was a *thing* and the egg I was carting felt heavier than my pack.

After five days of hard slog it was a bit of an anticlimax bursting from the bushes into the carpark and seeing the muddy school bus. I'd found my walking rhythm by then and looked forward to that moment of euphoria when I finally shed my pack at the end of each day. Drunk and weightless, just for a few minutes. It wasn't much more than a sigh of relief when I dropped my bag beside the others in the shade of the trailer.

I was fifth to arrive. Not that it was a competition or anything, but Dana Quinn and Mena Karapanagiotidis were first back. Mena, hands on her hips, explained that she and Dana had touched the trailer at *exactly* the same time.

'*Exactly* the same time,' Parko concurred. 'Saw it with my own eyes.'

Mitch was next, then me. The five of us stood in a circle, all lycra skins and BO.

'You made it, guys!' Parko said. 'Well done.'

'Thanks,' Dana said, and hugged her.

Maybe there was some euphoria still in my blood after all, because I hugged Parko too. It didn't feel awkward until I'd let go, and then only for a split second until Mitch put his arms around her. Parko's body sounded like a drum as he thumped her back.

→

Parko unlocked the bus. I climbed in the trailer and stacked the packs as they arrived. Tariq thanked me under his breath but couldn't look me in the eye. That was weird. Tariq is normally a mouth on legs. Wim didn't even say thanks. Aaden carried his pack *and* Mikayla's. They were last to arrive, and I snapped the tailgate shut after their bags were stowed.

Aaden stood there, twirling his baseball cap in his fingers.

'Well done,' I said, and opened my arms.

His brow wrinkled and he drew his head back, then his face split with a smile like a sunrise and he stepped into my embrace.

'Well done you, Jack. We survived, hey?'

➳

We stopped at Macca's around the corner from school, but I stayed on the bus with Parko.

'Not exactly shiitake risotto in there,' she said.

'I'm not foodist,' I said. 'I forgot to bring money.'

'You want some? You can pay me back next week.'

'Thanks, but no. Maybe I am foodist after all?'

She snorted.

I'd almost dozed off when Dana tore the sliding door open again. They set the bus rocking as they piled aboard. Aaden stood beside my seat, digging in his paper bag. He pulled out a cheeseburger and small fries and held them out to me.

'Serious?'

He nodded.

I took the food. 'Thanks, man.'

He pinned the bag under his arm, made prayer hands and bowed at me. 'Thank *you*, man.'

And there it was again – that taste of naughty white wine.

One of the many flavours of love.

ACKNOWLEDGEMENTS

James Roy's gutsy interwoven short stories in *Town* and *City* paved the way in my heart for this work. Lots of little yarns can end up being a bit of a plate-juggling exercise for a writer but even more so for an editorial team. Thankfully Hilary Reynolds, Erica Wagner and Eva Mills are headline acts in the editorial circus of life, and they turned this pile of crockery into 'ta daaaa!'. I spent a few years supporting outdoor education camps with Kurnai College in Gippsland and I owe a deep debt of gratitude to Alan 'Schacky' Schack and Andy Leeson for the opportunities they sent my way. They modelled life off the map and set up the richest educational experiences I've been part of. I know they'd recognise many of the characters, settings and hardships fictionalised here. Ruth Slinn, an Airbnb host in Wagga, and her five-year-old son Nicholas shared the most cracking (and unexplainable) ghost story. My time with them inspired the piece 'Bad Billy'. 'Thingless' grew out of a roadside meeting with the modern-day swagman John Cadoret and later blossomed into characters and ideas explored in the novels *Sparrow* and *Changing Gear*. Anita Jonsberg developed the teaching notes for the collection and inspired 'The Wave'. Barry Jonsberg read early drafts and applied his signature seasoning of courage. As far as mates go, they're golden hen's teeth.

➳

A version of 'The Tunnel' was first published in 2009 by Pearson NZ with illustrations by Dean Proudfoot. 'Thingless' first appeared in the anthology *Rich and Rare*, edited by Paul Collins (Ford Street, 2015). 'Answers' was included in the *Trust Me* anthology edited by Paul Collins (Ford Street, 2008). An iteration of 'Another Theory of Evolution' was featured in *Where the Shoreline Used to Be: An Anthology from Australia and Beyond*, edited by Susan La Marca and Pam Macintyre (Penguin, 2016).

ABOUT THE AUTHOR

Scot Gardner became a writer after a chance meeting with a magazine editor while hitchhiking in eastern Australia. Magazine articles led to op-ed newspaper pieces and eventually novels. Scot's first fiction for young adults, *One Dead Seagull*, was published after he attended a writing conference with John Marsden.

More than a decade later, his many books have found local and international favour and garnered praise and awards for their honest take on adolescent life. They include books like *White Ute Dreaming* and *Burning Eddy* and most recently *Changing Gear*, shortlisted for the CBCA Book of the Year Awards; *Happy as Larry*, winner of a WA Premier's Book Award for young adult fiction; and *The Dead I Know*, winner of the CBCA Book of the Year Award for Older Readers.

Scot lives with his wife in a vegetable garden in country Victoria.

scotgardner.com

'Scot Gardner's descriptions of the Australian landscape, as expressed by Merrick, feel so real that at times you hardly dare to breathe, so overwhelming is the absurd beauty of it. It makes you want to laugh and cry and lie down in the dirt to become a part of it.'

DANI SOLOMON, Readings Kids